Dear Diary,

Today was a great day! First of all, I weigh 120 – hooray! I am so happy! The sweet taste of success (no pun intended). I'm still more than ten pounds fatter than Nancy Pratt, but at least I'm losing my chipmunk cheeks and my waistline looks pretty good. I still have a potbelly and ridiculous thighs, though. Think Mom would let me get liposuction, dear Diary? Fat chance!

from The Women's Press

Lesléa Newman is a writer and editor with over twenty books to her credit including *SomeBODY To Love: A Guide to Loving the Body You Have*, *Eating Our Hearts Out: Personal Accounts of Women's Relationships to Food*, *Every Woman's Dream*, and *Heather Has Two Mommies*. Her literary awards include a Massachusetts Artists Foundation Fellowship in Poetry and a *Highlights for Children* Fiction Writing Award. She lives in Massachusetts.

Fat
Chance

Lesléa Newman

Published in Great Britain by Livewire Books, The Women's Press Ltd, 1996
A member of the Namara Group
34 Great Sutton Street, London EC1V 0LQ

Reprinted 1999

First published in the United States of America by G P Putnam's Sons, 1994

British Library Cataloguing-in-Publication Data
A catalogue record for this book is available from the British Library.

ISBN 0 7043 4934 5

Printed and bound in Great Britain by Cox & Wyman Ltd, Reading, Berkshire

In memory of Deborah Slosberg
(1959–1990)

and for Janet

Fat Chance

Dear Diary,

Today was the first day of school and two things happened, one good and one bad. The good thing was Ms. Roth, our new English teacher, gave us all notebooks and said we were all required to keep a diary this semester, even the boys. She said all the great writers kept journals, like Sylvia Plath, who was this poet, I guess, and some writers even publish their journals but we don't have to worry about that. Ms. Roth says anyone who really wants to be a writer has to study his or her own life. That's what she said, "his or her." I don't know if I really want to be a writer or not, but for some reason I really like the idea of writing in a diary. I don't know what I want to be when I grow up and that's one of my goals for this year, to figure that out. My other goal is to have a boyfriend.

Ms. Roth isn't like any other teacher I've ever had before. She told us we had to read twelve books this semester, six that she assigns and six that we each pick out ourselves. Anything we want. "Why should everyone read the same books?" Ms. Roth asked. "You're not all the same." Our notebooks are all different, too. Ms. Roth brought in all kinds and spread them out all over her desk. Some were big, some were small, some had lined paper, some had unlined paper, and they all had different covers, too: red, purple, silver, one with Snoopy on it that nobody wanted, and some with designs. I wanted this shiny notebook with glitter all over the cover, but Nancy Pratt wanted that one, too, so I let her have it. Isn't it funny, dear Diary, that two people who are so different could both like the very same thing? I mean, Nancy Pratt is thin and beautiful and looks like she spent the entire summer vacation working on her tan and bleaching her hair, and I'm, well, I'm not too sure how to describe myself, but pale and dumpy-looking are two words that come to mind.

Anyway, not getting the notebook I wanted wasn't the bad thing that happened (by the way, I took a green notebook with lined paper, which I really do like, Diary, so don't feel bad). No, the bad thing happened before school when I went to get dressed this morning. I didn't pick out my clothes last night because, well, I guess I thought maybe I had gained some weight over the summer, but I really didn't want to know. So this morning I put on my favorite black pants and I could hardly zip them up, even lying down flat on the bed and holding my stomach all the way in. But I did it and I buttoned the button, too. But then when I stood up, my stomach was hanging over the top of my pants and I looked awful. So I had to wear my other black pants which are kind of worn-out at the knee and my mom gave me a hard time about that because she doesn't want anyone to think we're paupers which is an old-fashioned word that means poor people, I guess. My mom's very sensitive on account of being a single parent and everything. She doesn't want people to think she can't support her family. She wanted me to wear one of my new outfits, but only nerdy kids dress up on the first day of school; everyone else pretends they really don't care.

Anyway, it wasn't the fight with my mom that upset me (I won anyway), it was the fact that now I know I am really, really FAT. Well, not as fat as Ms. Roth, our new English teacher, thank God, but still, if I don't do something about my weight, I'm definitely on my way. Ms. Roth seems like an okay teacher, I guess. She wants us to call her Ms. instead of Mrs. or Miss so we won't know if she's married or not, which is really dumb because all you have to do is look at her left hand to see that she's wearing a gold band around her fourth finger. Which is really strange because like I said, Ms. Roth is fat, the fattest teacher I've ever had, so who would want to marry her? Everyone knows guys like skinny girls, the skinnier the better. And to make things worse, Ms. Roth wore a blue-and-white-striped top with the stripes going across, which everyone knows makes you look fatter, and white slacks when everyone knows fat people shouldn't wear white. Tommy Aristo called her Ms. Roth the Sloth but luckily she didn't hear him. I mean, it's true that Ms. Roth should lose some weight, but still, there's no reason to hurt her feelings like that. I mean, maybe somebody should talk to her about her appearance in a nice way, or at least give her some fashion tips. Not Tommy Aristo, though. He was really obnoxious last year, and I guess he's going to be really obnoxious this year, too.

Anyway, that's my third goal for this year, to lose weight, especially after what happened this morning. I'm going to start a new diet tomorrow. I've been on diets before, but this time I'm going to be really serious about it. I tried to lose some weight over the summer in fact, but there wasn't anything much to do except sweat and eat ice cream. And my body got a lot bigger, too. Mom says it's because I'm becoming a woman and all that. I don't really like it.

You see, this is my last chance to lose weight because next year I'll be in high school and who wants to be a fat freshman? (I guess Ms. Roth would say a fat fresh-person.) I mean, we're in the same building and every-thing, the high school is just on the other side of these swinging doors, but still, it's a big step and I want to start out on the right foot.

Well, this was sure a lot of writing, and I don't even know if it's what we were supposed to write about or not. Maybe I'll ask Ms. Roth.

Bye for now, dear Diary,

Judi

Wednesday, September 7

Dear Diary,

Today some kids asked Ms. Roth if she wanted to read our diaries. She said no, because our diaries are a private place where we can write our most intimate thoughts and feelings. "You wouldn't write down how you *really* feel about things if you knew a teacher was going to read it, would you?" she asked, looking straight at us with her hands on her hips, and of course no one could argue with that. "But how will you grade us?" Paul Weinstein

4

asked. He's always worried that he'll get an A minus and then his father will kill him because he won't be able to go to Harvard like his father and grandfather did.

"At the end of the semester, everyone will write a summary of what he or she learned about him- or herself," Ms. Roth said. She always talks like that. "Even if you come up with only one true insight about yourself, your diary will have been a success."

Now that is really dumb. I'm sure no one is going to keep a diary. They'll just write a one-page summary and hand it in in December. Ms. Roth is nice, but I can tell she's the kind of teacher kids take advantage of. She's new around here and somebody should really show her the ropes. I mean, Nancy Pratt even did her nails in class today and Ms. Roth didn't say a thing about it. Everyone noticed and I could tell they were all thinking about what they can get away with: passing notes, writing letters, you know, the usual stuff. Maybe Ms. Roth is so nice because she thinks no one really likes her because she's fat. I'm sure she's jealous of how Nancy Pratt looks (who isn't?). Ms. Roth has no fashion sense at all. Today she was wearing a bright orange dress with a big belt around her waist (or where her waist would be if she had one) and she looked like a giant pumpkin. What a fashion disaster. I mean, I couldn't help feeling just a little bit sorry for her. Now I, on the other hand, would never wear a dress as bright as that. I always wear black or brown or navy blue like you're supposed to if you have a "full figure" like I do, even if I am only in the eighth grade. And I always wear baggy clothes to hide all my lumps and bumps. Sometimes I think I want to be a fashion designer because I know a lot about what makes a person look good from reading *Seventeen* magazine all the time. Like I would tell Ms. Roth that orange is definitely not her color, and she should stay away from belts, especially wide ones like the one she's wearing today. I don't know, though. You have to be really attractive like Nancy Pratt to be in the world of fashion, even to be a designer, and I'm just not. Nancy Pratt is definitely going to be a model someday. Everyone knows she wants to be one, but her mother won't let her try out until tenth grade when she's sixteen. I don't want to be a model, really, but maybe more like a beauty consultant or something, you know, someone who tells other people how to look good.

Everyone has their good points (everyone but me, that is). Even Ms. Roth. She has curly brown hair and a nice-shaped nose. She's actually kind of pretty even if she does have two chins. Oh my God, I would die if she ever read this, but she told us she's not. She said writing in a diary is something you do for yourself, for your own personal growth. I could do with a little less personal growth, if you know what I mean, dear Diary. I'm already five feet four inches, which is taller than practically every boy in my class, and I already weigh 127 pounds, which is seven pounds more than I should, according to *Seventeen* magazine.

You see, you're supposed to weigh 100 pounds if you're five feet tall, and add five more pounds for every inch. So I should weigh 120 pounds, but I'd like to get down to 115. That would give me a little leeway, in case

I gained a pound or two. Which reminds me of a joke: "What's a leeway?" "Oh, about six or seven pounds." Get it?

Anyway, maybe I'll ask Ms. Roth if she wants to borrow my old *Seventeen*s sometime, so she can learn how to dress better. I wonder what her husband thinks. Maybe her wedding ring's a fake. Maybe she wears it just so we won't feel sorry for her.

Till tomorrow, dear Diary,

Judi

Thursday, September 8

Dear Diary,

Well, I guess some other kids are keeping diaries, because everyone had questions about them today. Nancy Pratt, who by the way was wearing the shortest black miniskirt I've ever seen, wanted to know how long it has to be each time we write (she's so lazy, all she ever thinks about is boys). And Richard Weiss wanted to know if Ms. Roth would give us some ideas of what to write about. Richard Weiss is nice, dear Diary. He's smart, but he's not nerdy like Paul Weinstein, even though they hang out together, and he has a sense of humor, but he doesn't tease people like Tommy Aristo, who's such a brat. And besides that, he's really cute. I think I kind of maybe like him, BUT DON'T YOU DARE TELL A SOUL!

Anyway, Ms. Roth said, "Your diary is unique, just

7

like each of you, so it would defeat the purpose if I said each entry had to be a certain number of pages long. Everyone must decide how much he or she wants to write." Everyone groaned when she said that, but then she said if we *really* wanted, she would come up with a list of questions to get us started, and everyone clapped. She said she would hand them out next week and meanwhile we should just write about whatever we feel like.

I'm going to write in my diary every day and see what happens. Maybe this is what Mom means when she says my life is an open book! That's what she always says when I tell her I don't know what I want to be when I grow up. I hope this year I find out.

Anyway, otherwise it hasn't been such a good week after all. Remember I said I was going to start a new diet on Wednesday? Well, Tuesday night I decided I could have two Oreo cookies, since I wasn't going to have any cookies or candy or anything like that for a really long time, and Oreos only have 51 calories in them anyway. I looked them up in my Brand Name Calorie Counter.

Anyway, the best way to eat Oreo cookies is to pry them apart so all the cream is on one chocolate cookie half. Then you put two creamy halves together and voila! You have a double Oreo (I know you could just buy a package of Oreo DoubleStuf but that would be cheating). I'm usually pretty good at it, but on Tuesday night for some reason, it took me like ten times before I could get two Oreos separated right. And of course

I had to eat all the mistakes, you can't just put them back.

So before I knew it, I ate 510 extra calories. Sometimes I think I should be a mathematician because I can figure out the calories of any food and add them up just like that. But I don't know, math is so boring. Anyway, after I ate the Oreos, I decided I might as well really pig out and eat anything that was going to tempt me, since I absolutely have to stick to my diet from now on. So while Mom was in the living room drinking her coffee and watching TV, which is what she does every night after supper, I ate a bagel and cream cheese, a peanut butter sandwich, and a vanilla ice cream bar. I felt kind of sick after that, so I just went upstairs and did my homework.

On Wednesday I was pretty good all day, but I wound up eating more Oreos after supper. I hate to admit it, dear Diary, but I finished the whole box!

Today finally I was good. I had half an English muffin for breakfast with just a little bit of butter—that's about 100 calories—and a vanilla yoghurt for lunch, which is exactly 200 calories (it says so on the container). For supper we had flank steak and string beans and baked potatoes. I only ate half my potato and I didn't put any butter on it.

Now I'm in my room and I'm going to stay up here all night so I won't be tempted to eat. I have homework to do anyway, and I have to pick out what I'm going to wear tomorrow.

Not that I have a million outfits to choose from like

I'm sure Nancy Pratt does. I hate my clothes. They're all size 11/12. Last year I wore a size 9/10 but when Mom took me shopping for new school clothes in August, when there were all these back-to-school sales, we found that I went up an entire size. Mom wasn't really mad but I could tell she wasn't exactly thrilled about having to buy me all new clothes. At first I only picked out two skirts and three sweaters to mix and match, which Mom says is very stylish *and* economical, but then, since I'd gone up a whole size, we decided I probably needed more clothes than that. So I wound up with three big shopping bags and Mom had to pay with her charge card instead of a check, which I know she hates to do. She doesn't say anything but she gets these tight little lines around her mouth when she signs the sales slip.

Anyway, that's when I decided I had to go on a diet once school started. I mean, what if I go up an entire size every year, dear Diary? What if I wear a size 11/12 in eighth grade, a size 13/14 in ninth grade, a size 15/16 in tenth grade, a size 17/18 in eleventh grade, and A SIZE 19/20 IN TWELFTH GRADE? I'LL JUST DIE!

Anyway, I picked out my maroon V-neck sweater for tomorrow, which I'll wear with my black denim skirt. The skirt's a little tight around my hips, but the sweater is baggy and long so it'll cover what needs to be covered. Sometimes I wish I could just wear a big bag around my body and hide the whole thing.

Love,

Judi

Dear Diary,

Today Nancy Pratt raised her hand and said, "Ms. Roth, do we *have* to write in our diaries over the weekend?" like she was doing the whole class a big favor by getting us all off the hook. I'm sure Nancy Pratt will be too busy to write—she probably has a date Friday night *and* Saturday night, unlike some people like yours truly who have nothing better to do than baby-sit. Anyway, Ms. Roth said, "Nancy, you don't have to write in your diary over the weekend, even real writers give themselves a day off once in a while. But if anything really exciting or interesting happens, feel free to write it down." That sure made Tommy Aristo snicker. He said in a whisper loud enough for everyone to hear, "But Ms. Roth, you didn't tell us our diaries could be X-rated." Nancy Pratt just ignored that comment and so did Ms. Roth. She was wearing this white blouse which was pretty see-through—you could see the white lace of her bra if you looked hard enough—and a tight purple skirt. I mean Nancy Pratt was, not Ms. Roth. Can you see Ms. Roth in an outfit like that, dear Diary? Fat chance.

While we were doing our assignment, Nancy Pratt was looking at this modeling magazine she was hiding behind her notebook. I couldn't read it, but I could see some of the pictures. Some of the girls in the magazine are so skinny, they're even thinner than Nancy Pratt! They all have beautiful hair and perfect smiles and it's really depressing to know I'll never be pretty like that.

11

I'm not pretty and I'm not smart, so what am I? Most people are either one or the other. I don't even like most of my other classes, which is why I haven't written anything about them. English is the only class I like, the rest are really boring. In science we're doing biology, in social studies we're doing the Civil War and current events, in French we're conjugating verbs, and in math we're doing word problems. Oh, and then there's gym of course, which I almost forgot and which I wish I could forget. I hate gym. My locker is right next to Nancy Pratt's so I try to turn my back so she won't see my flabby stomach when I change into my gymsuit, but that just means she can see the rolls of fat around my waist. Not that Nancy Pratt noticed me or anything, Diary, but I sure noticed her. Her body is perfect. She's thin everywhere except her boobs. She was wearing jeans today (skintight, of course) and when she took them off, they didn't even leave marks on her belly, the way mine always do. Some people have all the luck, I guess. Nancy Pratt knows she's lucky, too. I mean, why else would she just stand there in her pink lace bra and matching underwear, brushing out her hair? The rest of us jump into our gymsuits as fast as we can, but Nancy Pratt takes her own sweet time. I'm sure she knows that everyone is watching her and admiring her. Oh well. If I looked that good, I'd probably be a show-off, too.

Till tomorrow, dear Diary,

Judi

Dear Diary,

Today I got brave and decided to weigh myself. One hundred and twenty-eight pounds. I don't know how I could have gained a pound. I've been good since Thursday, but I guess I wasn't so good in the beginning of the week.

Today I went over to Monica's house and hung out with her most of the day. Monica's my best friend. She moved here last year and everyone liked her right away. She could have been best friends with anyone, but for some reason she picked me. I don't know why. Probably because I only live two houses down from her and she didn't know any better. Monica's going to be a musician when she grows up. She plays the piano and the flute and she has perfect pitch. She can listen to a song only once and then play it on the piano like she's practiced it a hundred times. Monica plays classical music mostly, but sometimes she'll fool around and play regular songs we can sing along to. Just for fun, though. Monica has an okay voice, and I'm completely tone deaf. We would never sing in front of anyone except each other, of course. I definitely don't have what it takes to be a rock star!

Anyway, Monica's mom went out shopping and her dad works on Saturdays and her brother's away at college, so we had the whole house to ourselves and I only ate an orange for lunch. Monica asked me wasn't I hungry, and I told her my three goals: to lose weight, figure out what I want to be, and have a boyfriend (I didn't tell her about Richard Weiss though; that's still our secret, Diary). I asked Monica what her goals were and she thought about it while she ate her lunch. She ate a meatball sandwich and a brownie, and drank a glass of milk, which all adds up to 600 calories at least, but it doesn't matter because Monica has a great body. She can eat whatever she wants to and she still wears a size 7/8. It's not fair, but I guess life's not fair, which is what Mom always says.

"I guess I want to practice my music every day, kiss a boy for the first time, and have real boobs," Monica said after she finished her milk.

"You have a great body," I told her as she washed her dishes. "Besides, anything over a handful's a waste anyway, according to Nancy Pratt."

"She should know," Monica said, and we both laughed. Last year Nancy Pratt went to second base with Kevin White when she was going out with him. At least that's what he told Tommy Aristo who told practically the whole school and then Nancy Pratt broke up with Kevin White, so it must have been true.

Anyway, once me and Monica did the pencil test, you know, where you put a pencil under your boob and if it stays you need a bra, and if it falls out you don't? We read about it in *Seventeen*. Well, when I put the pencil under my breast, it stayed, of course. I mean, I could probably hold a pencil, a pen, a ruler, and Monica's flute under there. When it was Monica's turn, the pencil fell. Twice. Both boobs. She said I was lucky I got to wear a bra, and I said she was lucky she didn't have to. I guess that's what Mom means when she says the grass is always greener.

Like our hair. Monica wishes she had curly hair like mine (only it's not curly, it's frizzy) and I wish I had straight hair like hers. That's what we did all afternoon, tried out different hairstyles on each other. I washed Monica's hair in the sink and braided it into like twenty little braids when it was still wet. Then when it was dry, I unbraided them and it looked like Monica had a perm! Maybe I'll be a hairdresser when I grow up. I think I'm pretty good at it, but it's kind of scary. I mean, what if you cut someone's hair real short and then they don't like it? You can't just paste it back on. I guess it would always grow back, but still, they'd be awfully mad.

Anyway, after I did Monica's hair, she ironed mine with a towel over it so it wouldn't burn. I read that beauty tip somewhere and I've always wanted to try it, because I can never blowdry all the frizz out. Anyway, my hair came out pretty straight except for this one ridge near the top, but I didn't want Monica to get too close to my head. I mean, what if she fried my brain?

So then Mrs. Pellegro came home and she said to Monica, "Hi, Judi. Monica has a green sweater just like the one you're wearing, isn't that a coincidence?" and then she said to me, "Monica, can you help me put these groceries away?" so I guess our hairstyles were a real success. I mean, Mrs. Pellegro didn't really mix us up, but still, she got the right idea. Anyway, then Mrs. Pellegro invited me to stay for supper but I had to go baby-sit, which is lucky because they were having lasagne and Mrs. Pellegro is a great cook. I think we're just having hamburgers and I better go because Mom just called me.

See ya,

Judi

Dear Diary,

I am so disgusted with myself. I weigh 129 pounds and I look like an elephant. I swear, if I wore a gray pair of pants and a gray top, they would definitely put me in the zoo.

What happened is this. I pigged out last night at the Aaronsons' house where I baby-sit. Before Mr. and Mrs. Aaronson left, they gave me like a million phone numbers in case there was an emergency, and then Mrs. Aaronson said, "Help yourself to whatever you want, Judi, you know where everything is." I sure do, dear Diary. I really wish Mrs. Aaronson would say, "Now, don't eat us out of house and home, Judi," or something like that. Then maybe I'd be able to behave myself.

But me behave myself? Fat chance. Everything was okay while Eric and Michelle were still up. I helped them get into their PJ's and read them stories and made some shadow puppets on the wall for them, which they really liked. Maybe I'll be a kindergarten teacher when I grow up—everyone says I'm good with kids. I don't know, though, that doesn't seem very exciting.

16

Anyway, once Eric and Michelle were sleeping, there wasn't all that much for me to do. I mean, I brought my homework along, but that was just too depressing, to be doing French grammar on a Saturday night. I mean, Saturday night is supposed to be date night, everyone knows that. I'll probably never get asked out on a date. I'll probably spend every Saturday night of my entire life watching other people's kids so they can go out and have a good time. And what am I doing while everyone's out partying away? Eating, of course. Mrs. Aaronson keeps the place stocked with everything: pretzels and potato chips and Tootsie Rolls and ice cream . . . you name it, it's there. And boy, did I eat. I was careful not to open any new packages and I took all my wrappers home with me so they wouldn't know.

But oh, Diary, I am so fed up with myself. I have absolutely no willpower. I don't understand it. I'm pretty good during the day, but at night I just can't seem to control myself. I'm like Dr. Jekyll and Mr. Hyde, or should I say Ms. Hyde? To tell you the truth, I'd just like to hide, period.

But that's not even the worst part, dear Diary. The worst part is when Mr. Aaronson gives me a ride home and pays me. I feel so bad then, I feel like telling him to just keep the money, since I just ate like a hundred bucks' worth of groceries anyway. But of course I never say that.

So today me and Monica were going to go to the mall, but I called and told her I didn't feel so good. I mean, who wants to try on clothes when you're a blimp like me? Monica said it was just as well since she had to practice anyway, and I could come over if I wanted to. But to tell you the truth, dear Diary, I feel too fat to even leave the house.

Love,
Your FF (fat friend),
Judi

Monday, September 12

Dear Diary,

Today we had a surprise quiz in math, which wasn't fair at all—it's only the second week of school! And Tommy Aristo snapped my bra strap at the bus stop—he is so obnoxious! Thank God Richard Weiss wasn't there to see, even if Paul Weinstein was. He had his nose stuck in a comic book, but I know he saw. I hope he doesn't tell Richard Weiss—I would die! I wonder why no one ever snaps Nancy Pratt's bra strap—you can see it stretched across her back in a wide white stripe clear as anything under her cream-colored bodysuit. When Tommy Aristo wasn't listening, I said to Monica, "See why it's better not to have to wear one?" but she just shook her head. At least I stuck to my diet. Otherwise the day wasn't so hot.

Love,
Judi

18

Dear Diary,

This morning I weighed 128 pounds, so I'm happy about that. I've been eating half an English muffin for breakfast and a vanilla yoghurt for lunch and then a small serving of whatever Mom makes for supper. Maybe I should be a dietician—I could help other people lose weight by telling them what to eat. Or what not to eat is more like it. I wish I could just have a salad for supper, but Mom would never let me. She thinks eating three balanced meals a day is very important. Luckily since she got her promotion at the insurance company, she leaves for work before I leave for school so she doesn't know what I have for breakfast. We had a long talk about it when she was deciding to take the job.

"Judi," she said, "if I take the office manager position, I'll have a lot more responsibility, and that means you'll have a lot more responsibility, too. You'll have to get yourself off to school in the morning and look out for yourself after school until I get home at 5:30. Do you think you can handle that?"

Of course I told her yes—after all, I am almost fourteen. And even though it's kind of lonely in the morning sitting at the kitchen table all by myself, I know we need the money and I know Mom likes her new job. And there's an added bonus: I can skip breakfast during the week, which Mom would never let me do if she was home.

Lunch is never a problem because I eat at school. I

always eat with Monica. She's not in any of my classes, but at least we can eat lunch together. I wish I had enough nerve to plop my tray down right next to Richard Weiss and eat lunch with him. But knowing my luck, I'd probably dribble yoghurt down the front of my shirt and look like an idiot.

I wonder what Richard Weiss is writing in his diary. I wish I could read it, even though I would die if he read mine! I'm sure he's not writing about me. If he's writing about anyone, I'm sure it's Nancy Pratt, every boy's dream. Today she was wearing pants that were so tight, I'm sure she had to sew herself into them. I read once that that's what they had to do to Marilyn Monroe, sew her into her gowns and then rip out the seams at the end of the evening. I wonder how she sat down. Nancy Pratt sits down just fine and then all the boys sit down right next to her. I wonder who she'll go out with this year. I don't really care, as long as it's not Richard Weiss.

Love,
Judi

Wednesday, September 14

Dear Diary,

Not much happened today. I'm still holding steady at 128 pounds, Richard Weiss still hasn't said a word to me, and I still don't know what I want to be when I grow up. So much for my goals! I guess there's still time to work on all three. I just think if I lost some weight, everything else would work out, too. I can't believe I still weigh 128 pounds. I made sure the scale said zero when I wasn't standing on it, and then I moved it to the middle of the floor instead of up against the wall, but it still said 128 when I got on. And not only that, but when I moved the scale I saw there were dust bunnies everywhere, so I had to clean the bathroom. It's my responsibility since I'm the only one who uses it. Mom has a bathroom attached to her bedroom, so we each have our own. Mom even let me pick out the colors to decorate my bathroom with. I chose very, very light blue paint for the walls, and white linoleum with pink-and-blue specks in it for the floor. Then Mom let me buy my own towels too, to match.

Anyway, I'm really getting frustrated about my poundage problem. I wish I could get one of those operations where they take out part of your intestine and then you can eat whatever you want without gaining any weight. Could you see Mom letting me do that, dear Diary? Fat chance! She says I need all my nutrients because I'm a growing girl. Yeah, I'm growing all right—sideways!

Tonight Mom said we should call Grandma and Grandpa to wish them a happy Rosh Hashanah. Rosh Hashanah starts tomorrow night at sundown and my grandparents are pretty religious. They won't answer the phone on the holiday, which is why we have to call them a day early. So Mom called. First she had to talk to Grandpa. I can always tell when she's talking to him because she has to talk LOUD on account of his hearing aid and they always argue about money. I guess Grandpa wanted us to come down to Florida to see them for the holiday and Mom said we couldn't afford it, so he said he would pay for it and she said she didn't want his money. She kept yelling, "We don't need any money. We're fine," which is really weird because of course we need money. I mean, we're not poor or anything, but Mom always buys stuff on sale and she's always cutting coupons out of the paper. Then she talked to Grandma and I couldn't really hear what she was saying because Grandma's hearing is fine so she doesn't have to shout. Grandma always asks Mom, "How's your social life?" which is her way of saying, "Are you dating anyone?" which she isn't. I know, because Grandma always asks me the same question, and I'm not either.

That's all for today, dear Diary. I'm sorry this is so boring, but my life just isn't all that interesting right now. Maybe something exciting will happen tomorrow.

Love,

Judi

Thursday, September 15

Dear Diary,

Guess what—something exciting did happen today! Maybe I should be a psychic when I grow up—you

22

know, one of those people who can predict the future. You'll never guess what happened, dear Diary, so I'm just going to tell you: Richard Weiss smiled at me. He really did! I even have a witness: Monica. We were walking down the hall after lunch and we were late because Monica forgot her flute so we had to go back to her locker to get it. So then we were walking the opposite way from everyone else and right when I wasn't even thinking about him, Richard Weiss just appeared out of nowhere coming right toward us, and just as we passed, he looked right at me and he smiled! You'd think he would smile at Monica, but no, he smiled at me, *at me!* Monica almost dropped her flute, she was so surprised. I had butterflies in my stomach for the rest of the day, and I couldn't even think about eating. I just have to lose weight soon so Richard Weiss will ask me out. Oh, Diary, what if we fall in love?

Love,

Judi

Friday, September 16

Dear Diary,

Today is Rosh Hashanah, so there's no school. I mean, there is school, but not for the Jewish kids. We get to go to temple instead. Rosh Hashanah is the Jewish New Year, and you're supposed to eat something sweet so you have a sweet year. Just my luck, huh, Diary? Well, speaking of luck, guess who was at temple, sitting two rows in front of me and Mom? Richard Weiss! He had a yarmulke pinned on his head with a bobby pin, and he was wearing a suit. He didn't turn around and see me, but I stared at the back of his head during the entire service. He's so cute, even from the back, dear Diary. And besides that, he's the only decent boy in the entire eighth grade. I hope I lose this weight fast so he'll ask me out soon. After temple, which was really boring by the way (at least I know one thing I don't want to be—a rabbi), we went over to Mrs. Gross's house (God, I would die if I had a name like that!). Mrs. Gross lives three blocks from us and she's one of Mom's best friends and we always celebrate the Jewish holidays with her. I didn't really want to go, but Mom said I had to. "What do you want to do, sit home and celebrate the New Year all by yourself?" she asked, and I felt like telling her, yes, that's exactly what I want to do, but of course I didn't say anything. I thought maybe, just maybe if I kept my mouth shut I wouldn't stuff any food into it, but I was wrong, wrong, wrong.

First of all there weren't any other kids at Mrs. Gross's house when we got there, except for Evie Gross, who's only eight, so there was nothing for me to do. I mean, I went upstairs and let Evie show me her stuffed animal collection for a while, but then she wanted to go downstairs and be with her mother, so I came downstairs, too, and guess who was sitting there, dear Diary? No, not Richard Weiss unfortunately, but Paul Weinstein. He looked really bored sitting there with all those

24

grown-ups and I could tell he was just waiting for his parents to decide they were ready to go home, which wouldn't be for a while, since people were still coming in the door and everything. So I went over and talked to him, even though he's kind of a nerdy type of guy, but still he must have some redeeming qualities; I mean, after all, he *is* Richard Weiss's best friend. We talked about school for a while, and then we didn't have all that much to say to each other. So after we sat there not saying anything for a few minutes, Paul Weinstein pulled a comic book out of his pocket and just started reading it. Well, Diary, there is nothing more boring than watching someone else read something, so I got up to find Mom to see if we could go, but Mrs. Gross stopped me and asked if I'd had some honey cake yet. I said no, thanks, but she said I had to have something sweet for the New Year and besides, she made it herself.

So I had a little piece and I told her it was really good, which it was, and then I was off and eating again. It always happens like that, dear Diary. I'm okay if I don't eat anything, but as soon as I start, I just can't stop. You'd think I'd be able to control myself in public, especially in front of Paul Weinstein. I mean, what if he tells Richard Weiss what a pig I am? I don't think he noticed anything, though, he was so into his comic book. Anyway, it's not like I ate the whole table or anything. I just had a piece of sponge cake and some challah, which is this fancy kind of Jewish bread that's really good, and two pieces of cinnamon babka, which is Mrs. Gross's specialty. Still, you're supposed to eat

25

something sweet so you'll have a sweet year, not ten things so you'll have a sweet decade!

Oh well, tomorrow's another day, dear Diary.

Love,

Judi

Dear Diary,

Today is still Rosh Hashanah, so we went to temple again. We're not really religious or anything, we just celebrate the holidays like Rosh Hashanah and Chanukah and Passover. Richard Weiss wasn't at temple today so it was really, really boring. And besides I was mad at Mom so I really didn't feel like sitting there next to her.

We had this fight this morning, see, because I wanted to wear what I wore yesterday—my dark purple dress—and Mom said I couldn't wear the same thing two days in a row, what would people think, that we were so poor I only had one dress? I told her no one would notice and besides, it's the only thing I have that looks good on me anyway.

"Nonsense," Mom said, "you have plenty of nice things." She went into my closet and pulled out this red dress that she made me buy last year, which I absolutely hate. And besides, it's gotten a little tight.

"Forget it," I said. "That makes me look like a fire engine." So then Mom told me to pick out something,

26

so I put on my black skirt and a black sweater and went downstairs, but Mom said I looked like I was going to a funeral and Rosh Hashanah is supposed to be a happy holiday, so I had to put on something else. Finally we compromised on my black skirt and a green sweater, but honestly, Diary, I'm almost fourteen years old, you'd think I'd be allowed to pick out my own clothes already. I don't tell Mom what to wear. And anyway, I don't care if everyone thinks I only have one dress—it's the only dress I look good in because it has an empire waist and that makes me look skinny. Or skinnier at least. Oh well.

Anyway, I forgot to say Happy New Year to you yesterday, dear Diary, so Happy New Year to you!

Love,

Judi

Sunday, September 18

Dear Diary,

It's not Rosh Hashanah anymore, but now it's the Days of Awe, which are the ten days between Rosh Hashanah and Yom Kippur, and they're supposed to be very special days when anything can happen. One thing that happens is God is supposed to decide if you get to live another year or not, and then mark it down in His big black book. I've been pretty good, I guess. I get all A's and B's at school and I try to help Mom around the

27

house as much as I can, especially since she got her promotion. I don't do anything dumb, like smoke cigarettes or drink beer. The only thing I do that's bad is I eat too much, and that's wasteful, especially when there are people all over the world starving to death.

I'm really going to be good on my diet starting today. The New Year is a good time to start, Diary, don't you think? We Jews are lucky, I guess. We get to make New Year's resolutions twice: once on the Jewish New Year and once on the regular New Year.

So I was good on my diet for breakfast and lunch, but supper was a disaster. I was upstairs in my room reading an article in my newest issue of *Seventeen* about a girl who spent her senior year being an intern for a senator and she got to live in Washington, D.C., and everything. It all sounded pretty exciting and I was thinking maybe that's what I should do except I'm not even interested in politics, when I smelled something frying. Sure enough, when I went downstairs for supper, Mom had made chicken cutlets and they were breaded and deep fried in oil and everything. I tried to cut around the breaded part and just eat the meat, but it was pretty impossible and I just ended up with a mess on my plate.

"What's the matter?" Mom asked. "Don't you like my cooking anymore?"

"It has nothing to do with your cooking," I said. "I'm on a diet."

"A diet?" Mom looked at me like I just said I was from Mars. "Why do you need to be on a diet?"

"Why?" I looked at her like she was from the planet Bimbo. "Because I'm fat, that's why."

"Judi, you are not fat," Mom said.

"Oh yeah? What do you call this and this and this?" I stood up and pointed to my hips, belly, and rear end. "Not to mention this," I said, grabbing my flabby upper arm. "I'll tell you what you call it—F-A-T, fat!"

"Don't be silly, Judi. You're just a growing girl," Mom said, even though I've told her a million times I *hate* when she says that. "You're developing very nicely and you don't need to go on a diet. Dieting isn't healthy at your age. You'll stunt your growth."

"Exactly!" I yelled. "That's the point, Mom. I'm too big already, and I'm only in eighth grade. I don't want to get any bigger."

"Judi, I'm sure you're going to grow up and be a very attractive young woman. You're just at an awkward stage right now. You'll grow out of it. Now, eat your dinner." She pointed at my plate and I gave in and ate, even though I really didn't want to. You see, dear Diary, I'm afraid Mom's right—I will *grow* out of this awkward stage into an even bigger, more awkward stage. I wish Mom would understand, but she doesn't. How could she? She's got a good figure. She has no idea what it's like to be the fattest girl in the entire eighth grade.

I wasn't the fattest girl last year. Sherry Polansky was. But her parents sent her to fat camp and she lost like thirty pounds in one summer. I wish I could go to a camp like that, but I'm not even going to bother asking Mom. Hey, maybe I could be a counselor at a fat camp. Mom would have to let me go if I was getting paid. But they would never hire a fat girl like me to be a counselor at that kind of camp. What kind of example would I be setting? I'm sure all the counselors there are as thin as Nancy Pratt. Oh well. Maybe Mom would let me go, but I doubt it. She just doesn't understand. And when I try to explain things to her, she just says, "Life's not fair," or "That's the way the cookie crumbles."

I wish me and Mom talked more, but we just don't. Mom works hard all day and when she gets home, she's really tired, even more tired than last year when she was just the assistant office manager. So she likes to come home and relax after supper with her feet up in front of the TV. And on weekends she's usually busy with grocery shopping and doing the laundry or going on her Mary Kay appointments (Mom sells Mary Kay cosmetics on the side to make some extra money). I'm usually hanging out with Monica or baby-sitting anyway.

So a little while later, Mom came up to my room to have a mother-daughter heart-to-heart talk. It was almost like she read my mind or something. Sometimes my mom is spooky like that. She calls it "women's intuition." Anyway, we're really not very much of a talking kind of family, but sometimes, like after we've had a fight or something, Mom decides we're like "ships passing in the night" and we should spend some quality time together, so she comes up to my room for a little chat.

So Mom stood in the doorway for a minute in her business suit and stocking feet with her arms folded, just looking at me. I was sitting at my desk, which is like my favorite thing in the world because it's this small, old, wooden rolltop desk with all these neat little shelves and drawers for me to put all my stuff in and it used to belong to my dad when he was a kid, besides. Anyway, I just kept pretending to do my homework, because I couldn't really concentrate with Mom standing there like that, and she wasn't saying anything and then finally she said in a casual voice, "So talk to me, Judi. What's new and exciting?"

"Oh, nothing really," I said without looking up from my homework. I mean, like I said, I wish me and Mom talked more, but when she tries to, it feels, I don't know, forced or something.

"Any B-O-Y's you want to tell me about?"

I laughed. "N-O!"

"How's school?"

"All right."

She walked over to my desk. "Need any help with your homework?"

"No, thanks."

Then we sort of ran out of things to talk about. I mean, I wish I could really tell Mom what's on my mind—my weight—but she made it clear at supper that she just doesn't understand. If I brought it up again, I'm sure she would just say something like, "Don't worry, Judi, I'm sure you'll turn out just fine." She just stood there and I felt bad that we had nothing to talk about so I asked her what was new with her and then I had to pretend I was interested in the baby shower they had for one of the women in her office today, and the new computer program that's giving her trouble. Anyway, after a while, Mom felt better because we had our little "talk," but I didn't. I don't know why I can't really talk to Mom, but at least now I have you, dear Diary, to tell all my problems to.

Love,

Judi

Monday, September 19

Dear Diary,

Today Ms. Roth gave me a pile of papers and asked me to hand them out and I almost died because that meant I'd have to hand one to Richard Weiss and I was so nervous that my hands would get sweaty or that the pages would stick together and I'd hand him two instead of one and he'd think I was an idiot, or worse yet, I'd drop the whole pile of papers when I got to his desk and then I'd have to bend over and pick them up right in front of him. But luckily, nothing like that happened. I just handed him one page like I was supposed to and he looked up and smiled and said, "Thank you," and I almost died. He has the most beautiful brown eyes I've ever seen, and he is so nice, not like all the other boys in my class who are so incredibly immature. Maybe it's because he has two older brothers who've taught him a thing or two. He's the total opposite of that brat, Tommy Aristo. When I got to his desk, he whispered, "Judi has cooties, Judi has cooties," like we're still in first grade or something, and he sits right next to Nancy Pratt, which made it even worse. I'm sure she heard, but she just went on filing her nails like nothing happened.

The last person I came to was Paul Weinstein. He sits in the back of the room and just reads comic books all period. When I got to him, he showed me this drawing he did. It was a caricature of Nancy Pratt doing her nails, and the way he had drawn her, she was skinnier than the nail file she was holding, and her nails were bigger than her head! It was pretty funny, but it just proves my point—all the boys are obsessed with Nancy Pratt, including Richard Weiss, I'm sure.

Anyway, I was so nervous, I didn't even look at what I was handing out until I got back to my desk, and guess what it was, dear Diary? Ms. Roth's questions to help us with our diaries. I'm going to answer them tomorrow, since I already wrote so much today.

Ms. Roth, by the way, wore a navy blue dress today, with a red-and-white scarf tied around her neck, which was very sensible, since everyone knows a nice scarf or a pretty necklace draws the eye away from the hips up to the face. Maybe Ms. Roth finally went and bought herself a copy of *Seventeen* magazine.

That's all for today, dear Diary.

Love,

Judi

Dear Diary,

I'm going to answer Ms. Roth's questions today. Here goes:

1) Who are you?

I am Judith Beth Liebowitz, but everyone calls me Judi. I used to spell my name with a *y* at the end, but I changed it to an *i* because I think it's more sophisticated.

2) What is your secret desire?

I have two. One is to be the thinnest girl in the entire eighth grade, and the other is to be Mrs. Richard Weiss.

3) What is your biggest fear?

I have two. One is that I'll never figure out what I want to be when I grow up, and the other, which is a more serious fear, is that I'll get as fat as Ms. Roth someday, or even fatter.

4) What will your life be like ten years from now?

In ten years I will be 23¾ years old, and I will be married to Richard Weiss, and we will live in a big, beautiful house and have two children, a boy and a girl, and they will both look just like their father and be absolutely gorgeous. Richard Weiss will have a really important job and make lots of money so we'll never have to buy anything on sale, and I'll probably stay at home with the kids, unless by then I'll have figured out what I want to do with my life, because I think I want to be more than just a full-time mom, even though I'm not sure what.

5) What were you like ten years ago?

This is a really dumb question, because ten years ago I was only 3¾ years old, and who remembers anything from when they were a baby? I'm going to skip this question, since Ms. Roth said the questions were just a guideline and we should only answer the ones that were of interest to us.

6) Of all the people in the whole world, who would you most like to meet? (Person can be living or dead.)

I would most like to meet my dad and I wish he was living, not dead, but no matter how hard I wish that, he's going to stay dead forever and ever. My dad was killed in a car crash by a drunk driver when he was coming home from work one day when I was a baby. I don't really miss him much. I mean, how can you miss someone you never knew? Mom misses him a lot, though. She misses him so much that she still cries every time she talks about him, and it's been almost twelve years. I wonder if I'll ever love anybody as much as that.

I don't know much about my father. I know a few things about him, like he worked in an architect's office and he liked to carve things out of wood for a hobby and he did all these relief carvings of birds like swans and pelicans and ducks that Mom has down in the basement. But I don't know any of the important things about him, like did he wake up grumpy or happy in the morning? Did he drink coffee or tea? Would he watch the news after supper with Mom if he was still here, or help me clear off the table and talk to me? You know, things like that. I don't really ask Mom about him a lot because, like I said, it makes her cry to talk about him. But I wish he was here so I could know him. I think about him sometimes, especially on Father's Day. And Mom says I look like my dad some—I'm big—boned like his side of the family.

I have a picture of me, my mom, and my dad that was taken right after I was born. I look like a big, fat baby Buddha or something, bald, with this big belly, but my parents look really happy, smiling right into the camera. My mom never smiles like that anymore. Maybe she would if she got married again. Once I asked her why she doesn't, and she said, "Your father was the love of my life. We had six wonderful years together and no-body could ever take his place. Besides, I'm too tired to go out after work, and too old to start over" (she's only 38). Then her eyes filled up with tears and she changed the subject. Like I told you, Diary, we're not really a talking kind of family.

Anyway, one thing I wonder is, Why did God decide my dad couldn't live another year? Did he do something bad? Mom says he didn't, and no one can understand the ways of God. She says when your time is up, your time is up, and that's that.

But there must be a reason. I mean, there were proba-bly lots of cars on the road that day—why did the drunk driver have to crash into my dad? Mom says it was just fate, whatever that is. I looked it up in the dictionary and it said, "the supposed force that predetermines events." All I could think of was that old movie *Star*

Wars, where they say, "May the Force be with you." The dictionary also said that fate is "your final outcome." That sounds kind of gloomy, huh, Diary? Do you think my final outcome is to be a fat girl with no boyfriend who doesn't know what to do with her life forever? The reason I'm asking is, I weighed 127½ this morning, and I've been really good. I wish I could just wire my jaw shut for a few weeks or something.

Oh well. Slow and steady wins the race, I guess. That's one of Mom's sayings. First things first. That's another one. First I'll lose weight, and then my other problems will be solved, I just know it.

Well, Diary, I'm too tired to answer Ms. Roth's last two questions today. I'll do them tomorrow.

Love,
Judi

Wednesday, September 21

Dear Diary,

Here are the last two questions:

7) What's the worst thing that ever happened to you?

Besides my father getting killed, which I wrote about already, the worst thing that ever happened to me happened today. First of all, it's Indian summer, which I absolutely hate because it's too hot to wear long sleeves and everyone gets to see your flabby arms. You should have seen Ms. Roth's flab wiggling around while she was writing on the blackboard. Tommy Aristo sang, "J-E-L-L-O, Jell-O!" like the TV commercial all through the entire class. He made Nancy Pratt giggle and I'm sure Paul Weinstein drew a sketch of Ms. Roth with arms like huge sausages. Richard Weiss didn't seem to be paying attention to any of this. I'm sure he has more interesting and mature things to think about.

Anyway, my gym teacher, Miss Wilson, had the brilliant idea that we should have gym outside and soak up a little vitamin D. Now, even if you have an incredible body like Nancy Pratt, you still look pretty awful in your gymsuit, and if you're fat like me it's a double disaster. We had to run past all the boys, and Tommy Aristo yelled out, "Judi has boobies, Judi has boobies." At first I thought he was saying, "Judi has cooties" like he always does and I didn't really care, but then I heard what he was really saying and I just wanted to die. I looked down and my boobs were kind of bouncing around as I was running. I guess I never really noticed before because it's not like I run very often. Another thing I know I don't want to be (or know I can't be, rather) is an athlete or a gym teacher. Maybe I'll figure out what I want to be by process of elimination.

Anyway, after Tommy Aristo said that, I folded my arms in front of my chest but he saw that, too, so he knows he got me. Why does he always have to pick on me, dear Diary? It's not like I'm the only girl in eighth grade with boobs. Nancy Pratt's got some and they're twice as big as mine, but you know no one's going to tease her about them. Anyway, if they did, Bruce Kaplan would kill them. They just started going out and Nancy Pratt swears they're in love. My mother would never let me go out with a tenth grader—not that any have asked. At least I know that Nancy Pratt's going to keep her hands off Richard Weiss, for the time being, anyway. So that's one less thing to worry about.

Anyway, at lunch I told Monica what happened and she said, "At least that's not as bad as what he's always saying to me: 'Hey Monica, are those two pimples on your chest?' "

I guess no matter what you look like, boys will always find something to tease you about, (unless you're Nancy Pratt, of course). "Oh well," I said, "like my mom always says, boys will be boys. I wonder why they never say girls will be girls?"

Monica shrugged her shoulders and spread some ketchup on her hamburger. "I don't know, but there's one thing I do know."

"What?"

"Next time Tommy Aristo teases either one of us, I'm going to hit him over the head with my flute." Monica took a bite of her hamburger. "No, wait," she said with her mouth full. "I can't."

"Why not?"

"Because his head's thick as a brick and I can't afford a new flute."

"Too bad." I stuck my straw into my diet Pepsi and took a long sip. I've got to lose weight soon—I am so sick of being teased. Monica's boobs will grow in, that's just a question of time. But I'll never be thin unless I stop eating. I just had a banana for lunch today along with my diet soda—that's only 103 calories altogether. Monica said she admired my willpower.

Love,

Judi

Thursday, September 22

Dear Diary,

I forgot to answer Ms. Roth's last question, which is:

8) What is the best thing that ever happened to you?

This is a hard question, but I would have to say that the best thing that ever happened to me was Monica moving two houses down and picking me to be her best friend. Me and Monica talk about everything and she's really great. She's pretty and smart and funny and she's really a talented musician. Sometimes I sit on the piano bench next to her and listen to her practice, and when she nods her head, that's my signal to turn the page of her music. Maybe that's what I can be, a professional page turner for Monica when she gets to play with a real symphony orchestra. Maybe someday she'll even play at Carnegie Hall!

I don't know why Monica picked me to be her best friend. Some of the popular kids like her and she could have been best friends with almost anyone, but she chose me. Maybe because I'm fat and ugly and wear boring, baggy clothes, so she looks really good by comparison when she stands next to me. I read somewhere that some girls are never friends with anyone who's skinnier or prettier than they are.

Today I was pretty good on my diet. Until supper, that is. Mom made spaghetti and meatballs and garlic bread. I swear, she makes the most fattening things she can think of, on purpose. I told her I wasn't hungry, and she said, "Young lady, sit down and eat your supper." So I had two meatballs, which I figure is about equal to one hamburger, and a tiny bit of spaghetti. Mom noticed I only ate a little spaghetti—she kept looking at my plate—but I refused to look up at her, so she let it go for once in my life. We talked a little bit about our days, neither of which was too exciting, and then she went into the living room to put her feet up and watch TV. I made her coffee and brought it in for her—that's my job, to make Mom her coffee and clean up supper so she can relax a little. I guess that's fair, since she cooks and everything.

Anyway, when I went back into the kitchen to clean up, you won't believe what I did, dear Diary. Instead of throwing out the leftover garlic bread, I ate the entire thing! Oh, I am so sick of myself! I don't know what's the matter with me—I can go almost all day without eating and then at night I just make an absolute pig of myself. I wish I could just run away and get my stomach stapled.

I better get back on track or Richard Weiss will never smile at me again, let alone ask me out.

Love,

Judi

Dear Diary,

Today I weighed 128 pounds again. I am such a blimp. At least it was kind of cold so I got to wear my maroon sweater, which covers my flabby arms. It's really beginning to feel like fall, and I hope we don't have another Indian summer.

Today at lunch, Monica and I sat two tables away from Paul Weinstein and Richard Weiss. I was drinking my diet Pepsi as usual and Monica was talking to me about her music teacher, but I wasn't really listening because of course I was looking over at Richard Weiss. He was looking at this big sketch pad that Paul Weinstein was showing him, which was probably full of his caricatures (God, I hope he didn't do one of me!). Every time Richard Weiss looked up I looked away because of course I would die if he knew I was watching him.

"Alien beings have surrounded the school, and we're all being transported to the planet Numbula at exactly 1:15."

"What?" I looked at Monica. "What are you talking about?"

"I just wanted to see if you were paying attention," she said, taking a bite of her chop suey.

"I'm sorry." I swiveled around in my seat so I was completely facing her. "I wasn't going to tell you this, but, um . . . well, I kind of like Richard Weiss and I was just, you know, looking at him."

"You think I don't know that?" Monica asked, and I could feel my cheeks turning hot, so I must have been blushing. God, I hope it's not that obvious to everyone, especially to Richard Weiss.

Monica looked over in his direction and then looked back at me. "Maybe he likes you, too," she said. "Remember he smiled at you that day in the hall? He never smiles at me."

See, dear Diary, how great Monica is? She didn't say, "You'll never get him," or "You and Richard Weiss? Fat chance!" which is what I really think. "Promise me you won't tell anyone," I said, and Monica laughed. "Who would I tell, Judi, my mother?" which is Monica's way of saying she doesn't have any other close friends except me, so what was I worrying about? I am so lucky to have her for my best friend.

My new goal is to weigh 120 pounds by Halloween. I know I can do it if I put my mind to it. Like Mom always says, "Where there's a will, there's a way."

Love,

Judi

Dear Diary,

Today it rained all day so I went over to Monica's house. I read my October issue of *Seventeen,* which came in the mail today, while Monica practiced, and then we watched this old Alfred Hitchcock movie which wasn't even scary. I like the way Alfred Hitchcock is in his own movies for like five seconds and you have to watch for him. I would do the same thing if I was a movie director, which is just one more thing I know I'm not smart enough to be when I grow up.

When I got home, Mom and I had supper, which wasn't too bad: hamburgers (I didn't have any rolls) and mixed vegetables and applesauce. Mom apologized that it wasn't a gourmet meal, but I told her it was fine and that I really liked it, in fact. I didn't tell her the real reason I liked it, of course—it's one of the least fattening meals she ever cooks. Now I have to go baby-sit at the Aaronsons' house. Mom's going to drop me off on her way to the movies. Talk about depressing—I'm probably the only kid in America whose mother has a more exciting social life than she does. I mean, going out with a bunch of girls from the office isn't like going out on a glamorous date or anything, but still, when we got into the car I couldn't help noticing that Mom was wearing a nice pair of gray slacks and a fuzzy pink sweater, and I was the one in an old pair of baggy sweats. What is wrong with this picture, I wanted to say, but of course I didn't. Instead I made a silent vow to myself that I, Judi

Beth Liebowitz, will not eat or drink anything except diet soda the entire night.

Love,
Judi

Dear Diary,

I blew it, I blew it, I blew it. I really am disgusted with myself. I weigh 129 pounds, which is more than I've ever weighed in my entire life. I swear, if I get up to 130 pounds, I'm going to run away and be a fat lady in a circus. At least that way I'll have reached one of my goals—I'll have finally figured out what I want to be when I grow up.

But I don't *want* to be a fat lady in a circus. I want to stop eating and I don't know how. I was fine last night at the Aaronsons' house until the kids went to sleep. Then I went back downstairs and watched TV like I usually do but nothing good was on so I shut it off and just sat there for a while. Then I tried calling Monica but she wasn't home. She didn't have a date or anything (she would have told me) so she was probably out with her parents getting ice cream at Friendly's or something. Monica's family is pretty close. They even made this corny message for their answering machine, with Monica playing the piano in the background and her father saying, "Hello. The lovely music you hear in the background is being performed by my lovely daughter, Monica Pellegro. If you are calling about her performance at Carnegie Hall, please leave a message and we'll get back to you soon." I told the machine I wanted two tickets for front-row seats and then I hung up. You never know what you're going to get when you call Monica's house. Last week the machine had Monica's mother on it saying, "You have reached Pellegro's Pasta Palace. Please place your order after the beep."

Anyway, while I waited for Monica to call me back, I thumbed through an old *People* magazine lying on the Aaronson's coffee table. There was this ad for frozen yoghurt and as soon as I saw it, I knew I was a goner. I tried to read some of the articles, but all I kept thinking about was that frozen yoghurt and how I wished I had some and how good it would taste. I couldn't stop thinking about it. I know this sounds crazy, dear Diary, but it was like these voices were coming out of the kitchen, saying: "Judi, I'm sure Mrs. Aaronson has some frozen yoghurt in the freezer." "Judi, come on into the kitchen, we're all waiting for you." "Judi, you know you can't resist." "Judi . . ."

Maybe I'm losing my mind, dear Diary. I tried to ignore the voices, but they wouldn't go away. I turned the TV on again to distract myself, but just my luck, a commercial for Keebler cookies was on! It's like the whole universe is out to get me and make me eat more and more food. I tried calling Monica again but she still wasn't home, so I just gave in and really pigged out big time. And then guess what happened: Mr. and Mrs. Aaronson came home half an hour early! I was eating this big bowl of mint chocolate chip ice cream (which is better than frozen yoghurt any day) when I heard Mr. Aaronson's key in the door and I didn't know what to do. So I just shoved the whole thing under the couch with the spoon and everything! Oh God, I sure hope Mrs. Aaronson never finds it.

Then, when Mr. Aaronson drove me home, I told him I couldn't baby-sit anymore. I didn't tell him why, of course, but he didn't really ask. He just said, "I guess you're getting to the age where you have more interesting things to do than baby-sit on Saturday nights." I wish! Then he gave me a five-dollar tip which was the worst part of all, since I owe the Aaronsons at least ten times that much in food. Oh well. Maybe now that I won't be trapped in their house with all that food I'll be able to stick to my diet.

I'm going to be really good from now on and I'm going to start exercising, too. They have these special sit-ups in *Seventeen* to "tighten your tummy" and some special leg lifts to "slenderize those thighs." I'm going to exercise every night before bed so I won't be tempted to eat.

Time for homework. See you, dear Diary.

Love,
Judi

Monday, September 26

Dear Diary,

Today is Yom Kippur so I went to temple instead of school again. Richard Weiss was already in his seat in

47

between his parents reading a prayer book, so I didn't get a chance to say hi. But at least I had something interesting to look at all during services, since he sat two rows in front of us again.

Yom Kippur isn't exactly my favorite holiday. It's the holiest day of the year, and you're not allowed to do anything. You can't read or watch TV or listen to music or talk on the phone or even eat, which is the only thing I like about this whole day. You're not supposed to eat or drink anything from sundown yesterday until sundown today. This is the first year I've done it.

After supper last night, Mom asked me if I was going to fast. "You're thirteen, which means in the Jewish tradition that you're a woman," Mom said. "But you don't have to fast if you don't want to, Judi. It's a really long day and you're a growing girl."

"But I want to fast," I said, ignoring her "growing girl" remark so she wouldn't know the real reason I was fasting—not for religious reasons, but to help me lose a pound or two.

"All right," Mom said, "but if you get really hungry, I want you to eat something before sundown. You don't have to be a martyr. And Judi," she looked me in the eye, "I'm proud of you. You're getting so big, I mean so grown up," (she must have seen me wince) "I can hardly stand it."

Dear Diary, if Mom only knew I'm getting SO BIG I can hardly stand it myself. But today's been really great. It's 3:00 already and I haven't eaten anything since yesterday's supper and I'm not even hungry. I bet I lost a whole pound or maybe even two. I wish Yom Kippur lasted two days like Rosh Hashanah, or even eight days like Chanukah. I wouldn't mind fasting for a whole week or even every day for the rest of my life!

I better stop writing, Diary, because I'm not supposed to be doing anything except sitting around and thinking solemn thoughts about everything I did last year and how I can do better next year. This holiday is really pretty boring.

So, Good Yontif, dear Diary. That means Happy Holiday, even if there isn't all that much that's happy about it.

Love,
Judi

Tuesday, September 27

Dear Diary,

Well, we went to Mrs. Gross's house to break the fast and everyone pigged out, including me. I didn't want to go of course, and I tried to tell Mom I didn't feel good, but I couldn't exactly say I had a stomach ache since I hadn't eaten all day, so I said I had a headache and of course Mom said it was from not eating and I'd feel a little better once I had some food in my stomach and we didn't have to stay very long. So I gave in and of course I ate too much. I swear, if Paul Weinstein ever drew a caricature of me, I'm sure he would draw a Miss Piggy

49

look-alike with brown frizzy hair. He was at Mrs. Gross's house, too, and we talked a little, but mostly I just *ate*. Mrs. Gross had enough food out to feed the entire junior high: bagels and challah and whitefish and Swiss cheese and egg salad and noodle pudding and sponge cake and cookies. And everyone kept saying how famished they were and eating and eating and eating, and Mrs. Gross just kept coming out of the kitchen with more and more food. It was like a nightmare!

Right before I left, Paul Weinstein showed me this cartoon he drew of Mrs. Gross up in the sky dropping all this food out of her apron like manna from heaven, and down below her all these tiny people were scurrying around like ants. I can't really describe it, but it was pretty funny. Paul Weinstein is really good at drawing.

"What should I call it?" he asked me.

"I don't know. 'Manna from Heaven'? 'Mrs. Gross's Feast'?"

Paul Weinstein shook his head. "No, it has to be funny, you know. This is a *cartoon*." He sighed. "That's always the hardest part. I can draw okay, but I can never think of the words."

I looked at the cartoon and thought for a minute. "I know," I said. "How about, 'The Hostess with the Most-est'?"

"Hey, that's great!" Paul Weinstein wrote it down at the bottom of the drawing and smiled at me. "Thanks, Judi."

Me and Mom left pretty much after that and as soon as we walked in the house, the phone started ringing.

Mom picked it up and I could tell right away it was my grandfather. "Of course I fasted," Mom said in a loud voice. Then she added, "Judi fasted, too, for the first time. Wait a minute, I'll put her on."

So then I talked to my grandfather and he was so proud of me for fasting, it almost made up for me not having a Bas Mitzvah last year. Grandpa and my mom had a huge fight over that one, but Mom said it was up to me and I didn't really want to do it. Anyway, then my grandmother got on the phone and told me how proud of me *she* was. They made such a big deal about it, they didn't even want to talk to Mom after they were done talking to me, and I could tell Mom was glad. She doesn't really get into religion the way my grandparents do. I think it's because she doesn't understand how a God that's supposed to be so kind and loving and everything could take my father away from us like that for no reason. I don't really understand it either.

Anyway, it's weird that everyone's so proud of me for not eating. I am really going to stick to my diet so they can be proud of me for that, too. Soon I'll be so thin and good-looking that Richard Weiss will definitely ask me out. Do you think, dear Diary, that I should become friends with Paul Weinstein? I mean, maybe he's a nerd, but I don't know, he's kind of a nice nerd, if you know what I mean. And he is best friends with a certain someone whose initials are R.W. But that would be kind of mean, wouldn't it, to sort of use someone like that.

I better just concentrate on my new regimen. I swear to you, dear Diary, that I, Judith Beth Liebowitz, will be good on my diet and weigh 120 pounds by Halloween or else!

Love,

Judi

Dear Diary,

An awful, awful thing happened in math class today. Mr. Jones asked me to go up to the blackboard and figure out this long division problem. I hate standing in front of the room with my back to the entire class like that. Luckily I was wearing a really long, baggy black sweater I could pull down over my fat rear end.

I was doing the problem, which was really complicated, so I had to write all the way down to the bottom of the blackboard, and just as I bent over, someone made this really loud farting noise and everyone laughed. I just wanted to die. I'm sure it was Tommy Aristo. One day I'm going to murder him, dear Diary, I swear to God. And the worst part of all is Richard Weiss is in my math class and now he'll never ask me out, even if I get down to 103 pounds, which isn't very likely, the way I'm going.

After class, Paul Weinstein ripped this piece of paper out of his notebook and gave it to me. It was a drawing of Tommy Aristo bent over backwards in this really impossible position, with his head between his legs, yelling something into a megaphone. I would love to see him looking really stupid like that. Paul Weinstein asked me what he should call it, and I knew right away: "Old Fart." Paul Weinstein thought that was really funny. Do you think I could get a job as a caption maker-upper, dear Diary? Paul Weinstein gave me the drawing to keep and I felt a little better, but not much. He said everyone was laughing at Tommy Aristo, not at me, but I don't believe him. I'm going to hang Paul Weinstein's drawing up and use it as a dart board.

I was so depressed today, I even told Mom what happened. I expected her to say her usual, "boys will be boys" or something, but she didn't. She said, "Just ignore him, Judi. He probably likes you and this is the only way he knows how to show it." Do you believe it, dear Diary? Mothers can be *so dumb*!

Love,

Judi

Thursday, September 29

Dear Diary,

Another disaster of a day. Today we had a bus drill, which is kind of like a fire drill, only a hundred times worse because everyone has to jump out of the bus through the emergency exit and there's no steps and it's really high.

Of course I was the next to last one off the bus and I

would have been the last one off if Monica hadn't asked me to go before her so I could hold her flute. Nancy Pratt went right before me and you should have seen her, dear Diary. She jumped down as graceful as could be, right into Bruce Kaplan's arms, just like a ballerina. Then he put her down and she looked around and smiled at everyone like they should all applaud. She's going to be a really great model, I'm sure, she just loves being the center of attention.

Not me, though. I was wishing everyone would just keep watching her, but they didn't. So then it was my turn to jump and everyone looked toward the bus. It was worse than the high diving board because at least even if you do a belly flop, you know you're going to land in the water. I just knew I was going to land splat! on the pavement and I did, of course. My books went flying and I ripped my pants leg and scraped my knee. It was awful. Mom says there's a silver lining in every cloud, but the only good thing I can think of in this situation is, at least I wasn't wearing a skirt that flipped up over my head showing everyone my underwear. Oh, and at least Richard Weiss takes a different bus to school, so he didn't see me make a total idiot of myself. Oh well. I guess that's something to be grateful for.

Anyway, after I got up I took Monica's flute so she could jump down and then we went into school. Monica said "Oh, Judi, just forget about it. Ten years from now when we're all grown up, we'll be rich and famous, and we won't even remember this stupid bus drill or anything else about today."

I know Monica said that to make me feel better, but it only made me feel worse. "You're going to be a famous musician, Nancy Pratt's going to be a famous model, Paul Weinstein's going to be a famous cartoonist, and what am I going to be?"

"I don't know," Monica said, so I told her.

"I'm going to be world famous for being the biggest klutz in the universe," I said, and Monica just shook her head. People who know what they want to be just don't understand what it's like for people who don't.

That's all for today, dear Diary,

Judi

Friday, September 30

Dear Diary,

Since it's the last day of the month, I decided to read over everything I've written so far, so I did and I learned two things:

1) I sure wrote a lot, and
2) most of it is awfully boring.

I guess I'll be able to write a one-page summary in December, but I don't know about finding any true insights about myself except that I'm really pretty boring and I don't think that's quite what Ms. Roth had in mind.

Oh well. I don't really know what to write in a diary. I've only read one diary before, *The Diary of Anne Frank*. Anne Frank was this Jewish girl who had to hide from the Nazis for a really long time, only then they found her and took her to a concentration camp. At least if I was in a concentration camp, I wouldn't have to worry about being fat. I know that's a horrible thing to say, but it's true. Looks are everything, dear Diary, it's just a fact of life. The pretty girls at school are the most popular. Everyone wants to be friends with them, and they're the ones that get asked out on dates. All the girls at school are obsessed with how they look. You should see the crowd in front of the mirror before the first-period bell rings. You can't really do much about your face though, if you're not born pretty, but if you're fat like me, the least you could do is stay on a diet and make an effort to look your best, even if your best isn't as good as everyone else's. I swear, Nancy Pratt looks better on her worst day than I do on my best day. Today she was wearing this lipstick that was more purple than red, and on anyone else (like me) it would look really stupid, but of course on her it looked absolutely perfect.

I wish I could be locked up somewhere away from food for a while. Not somewhere horrible, like a concentration camp or anything, but just somewhere quiet. Sometimes I wish I had diabetes, like this kid I once baby-sat for, Angeline. She wasn't allowed to eat any sugar at all, because it would make her sick. I wish sugar would make me sick, but all it does is make me fat!

I wish school was over already. It's only 2:30. I'm

sitting in math class and I'm writing in you, dear Diary, instead of working on my word problem. I mean, who cares if two trains are rushing toward each other at 110 miles per hour from Point A to Point B, so what time will they meet in Chicago? Here's the only word problem I care about:

> If a certain 13-year-old girl (her initials are JBL) weighs 129 pounds and she goes on a diet and eats only 800 calories a day, how many days will it take her to weigh 115?

Love,

Judi

Saturday, October 1

Dear Diary,

Happy October! It really feels like fall today. I love how crisp the air feels, and the leaves look really pretty, all gold and orange and red. And the best part of all is, it's definitely too cold for short sleeves—hooray! I am *so* glad that summer is over. Maybe by next June I'll be thin enough to wear a bikini instead of my stupid blue-and-orange striped one-piece that makes me look like a beach ball.

Anyway, I don't have to think about bathing suits yet (thank God!); after all, it's only October. Today me and Monica went to the mall because Monica has to get a black skirt and a white blouse for her music recitals.

They're not until December, but still she thought it would be good to get a head start and we couldn't think of anything else to do. So I watched Monica try on clothes and I tried not to stare at her body when she got undressed in the dressing room. I mean she's thin, dear Diary, but not too thin, you know, she just looks great and if I didn't like her so much (after all, she is my best friend) I'd probably hate her. It just isn't fair that she can eat anything she wants to and still wear a size 7/8.

Anyway, I kept running back and forth to the dressing room for Monica because she's really fussy about what she wears at her recitals. I guess I would be, too, if I had to be up there on stage in front of everyone, but I was getting pretty bored with all these plain black skirts that looked exactly the same to me. So just for fun I brought her a black miniskirt with holes cut out going all the way up the sides and she was so preoccupied, she didn't even notice until she had it on.

Monica turned and looked in the mirror and practically screamed when she saw herself. "Judi, are you nuts? I can't wear this to my recital! My music teacher would kill me!"

"Relax," I said. "It's just a joke. It doesn't look so bad."

"Yeah, if I was a contestant in a Nancy Pratt look-alike contest." Monica started walking around the dressing room swaying her hips from side to side. "Hi, big boy," she said to me, batting her eyelashes. "My name is Nancy Pratt. What's yours?"

"Bruce Kaplan. Wanna smooch?"

"Gross!" Monica stepped out of the skirt, got

dressed, and paid for two plain black skirts. I wanted her to get the sexy skirt for Halloween, but she said her mother wouldn't let her out of the house in it even as a costume. Oh well. I didn't try on anything, but I did buy a pair of silver hoops. Earrings are great—no matter how much you weigh, they always fit. Thank God for one thing—at least I don't have fat earlobes!

After all that, Monica was hungry, so we went and got her an ice cream cone and sat by the fountain so she could eat it. I must have looked pretty pathetic watching her because she asked me if I wanted a bite and I said no, thanks, because I was on a diet and then she asked me if I minded that she was eating an ice cream cone when I couldn't. I told her I didn't really care because during the day I don't really have so much of a food problem; it's mostly at night I have trouble, starting with Mom's fattening suppers.

Then I told Monica all about fasting on Yom Kippur this year for the first time and how I didn't feel hungry at all until we went to Mrs. Gross's house, and if Mom would have just let me stay home, I could have gone the whole day without eating.

"I wish I could just fast for an entire week," I said, watching Monica lick her ice cream cone. "Then I could just lose this weight once and for all."

"Why can't you?" Monica asked.

"You know," I said. "My mom. She makes me eat supper every night."

"So, tell her you ate at my house," Monica said, "Or tell her we went to McDonald's."

"Hey, that's a great idea." See what a good friend

Monica is, dear Diary? She always helps me figure things out. We're going to put Operation Fast into effect on Monday because tomorrow Monica has to go visit her cousins. I'm going to start doing my exercises, too.

You'll see, dear Diary, I'm going to get so thin, Richard Weiss won't be able to resist me, Tommy Aristo will stop bugging me, and Nancy Pratt will ask me to be her best friend.

Love,

Judi

Sunday, October 2

Dear Diary,

Today I had a whole English muffin for breakfast along with some orange juice but it doesn't matter since I'm going to start fasting tomorrow and I wanted to have a good breakfast like that in front of Mom so she wouldn't suspect anything. Mom asked me if I wanted to do something fun with her today and I told her no, I had to go to the library and get some books for my English class and she looked really hurt so I said we could watch the Sunday-night movie together, which is something we do sometimes. See, I wanted to go to the library to look up some books about fasting, dear Diary, and I found this really great book called, *The Fast Weigh Out*. I was kind of nervous that the librarian would get suspicious, so when I checked the book out,

I told her I was doing a paper on fasting for my science class. She didn't really say anything—I guess librarians don't talk much. Sometimes I think I wouldn't mind being a librarian. I mean, I like books and everything, but it doesn't seem too exciting. I guess I'll keep it in mind if I can't think of anything else.

Anyway, *The Fast Weigh Out* says that fasting is really healthy and it's a good way to get rid of all the toxins in your system (whatever they are). It also says that people fast for all kinds of reasons: to protest something like a war; to express their spirituality, especially Buddhists; and of course, to lose weight. When I got home from the library, I read the entire book and I can't wait to start.

Tonight after supper me and Mom ate some microwave popcorn when we watched the Sunday-night movie, which was a really dumb one based on a true story about this guy who had two families and of course neither one knew about the other one. So every time he visited one of his families he would put this stuff in his hair to make it curly and every time he visited his other family he would blowdry his hair to make it straight so no one would recognize him. It was pretty pathetic. "I could make a better movie than that," Mom said when it was over, and then she started goofing around. "I'm Mrs. Silverberg," she said in a squeaky voice, holding all her hair up on top of her head. Then she let her hair drop. "Now I'm Mrs. Goldberg," she said, lowering her voice. It was pretty funny.

Anyway, it doesn't matter about the popcorn I ate,

dear Diary, because that's it—that was my way of saying good-bye to fattening food forever. Before I went to bed, I adjusted the scale in my bathroom so I get a "true" reading of my weight tomorrow morning. I know it'll be bad, but it doesn't matter. After tomorrow, the number will just go down, down, down, I know it! So good night, dear Diary. I can't wait until tomorrow.

Love,

Judi

Dear Diary,

This morning I weighed 129½ pounds and I'm really glad I'll never weigh that much again in my entire life, except maybe when I'm pregnant, but thank God I don't have to worry about that at the moment! I've never even kissed a boy, let alone gone any further, and no boy is going to ask me out as long as I look like this, I'm sure. But watch out, Richard Weiss, before you know it, I'll be so skinny you won't even recognize me.

Today was the first day of Operation Fast and so far it's been a success. I put a bagel in the toaster oven before Mom left for work and then when she was gone, I wrapped it up in a napkin and stuffed it into my pocketbook so I could throw it out at school. Lunch was easy—I just sat with Monica and drank a diet Pepsi. Richard Weiss and Paul Weinstein sat one table over from us. I faced away from them so I wouldn't embarrass myself by staring. But every other minute I asked Monica, "Is he looking? Is he looking?" until she almost hit me over the head with her bologna sandwich, so I stopped.

Then all of a sudden, Monica sat up real straight, like a dog on alert or something, and looked over my head. "He's looking, he's looking," she whispered.

"Really?" I swear I could feel the hair on the back of my neck stand on end.

"He's looking, he's looking . . ." Monica paused. "He's looking at some of Paul Weinstein's comic books."

"Oh, you!" I picked up my diet Pepsi and threatened to pour it over her head but just then she smiled this really big smile and I turned around just in time to see Richard Weiss look away. "Did he smile at you?" I asked Monica.

"Yeah," she said, "but if you'd been sitting on this side of the table, he would have smiled at you," and I could have killed myself for not being brave enough to sit facing his table. All I got to look at besides Monica was a bird's-eye view of Nancy Pratt and Bruce Kaplan making goo-goo eyes at each other over their chicken chow mein for forty-five minutes—I bet they had a great weekend! Bruce isn't even supposed to eat with us. He must cut a class or something and sneak over here. And Nancy Pratt better watch it—chicken chow mein is pretty fattening. She's never going to be able to be a model if she keeps eating stuff like that. How she can eat such a big, fattening lunch and stay so thin is beyond me.

Anyway, after school I went over to Monica's house and stayed there until quarter to six (I left Mom a message on the answering machine so she wouldn't worry). Monica practiced her music and I just hung out. It's really soothing to listen to Monica play—sometimes she plays for hours at a time just because she likes to. I can't imagine liking something that much. I think everything's so boring.

Anyway, Mrs. Pellegro asked me if I wanted to stay for supper, but I said no, thanks, and then I walked the L-O-N-G way home, which is good because I burned up some extra calories. When I got home I told Mom I ate at Monica's and then I went upstairs and did my homework and my exercises. I can't wait to weigh myself tomorrow.

Love,
Judi

Tuesday, October 4

Dear Diary,

I weigh 127 pounds! Isn't that fantastic? I am so happy. My stomach was really flat when I woke up this morning. Aren't you proud of me?

At school there was an announcement during homeroom that tryouts for *Alice in Wonderland* are a week

64

from today and anyone who wanted to could pick up a script to study for the audition. A lot of kids think *Alice in Wonderland* is too babyish for eighth grade, but I don't know, maybe I'll try out. I wouldn't want to play Alice, that would be too scary, but maybe I could have a minor part. I don't want to be a professional actress or anything (though I wouldn't mind looking like Julia Roberts—ha, fat chance!) but maybe it would be fun to be in a play. Monica says I really should try out, I'm so dramatic and everything. She can't be in it because she's too busy with her music, but she said if I got a part, she'd help me with my lines. I decided I'd audition if I got down to 125 pounds by next Tuesday. I just can't go up on stage in front of everyone weighing any more than that.

When I got home tonight, I told Mom that me and Monica had eaten at McDonald's and I wasn't hungry. Mom got kind of mad at me for spoiling my appetite with junk food, but she believed me, which is the main thing. Two whole days with no food at all—this is great!

The only thing I don't like about fasting is this weird, dried-out taste in my mouth. It's like my tongue is made of sandpaper or something. In the book I took out of the library it says to drink lots of water and fruit juice so you don't get dehydrated but I'm just going to drink water and diet soda. I mean, an eight-ounce glass of orange juice has 120 calories in it, so what's the point?

Time for my exercises. I'm up to thirty sit-ups and

thirty leg lifts on each side. I'm going to do a few more every day and work my way up to a hundred.

Love,

Judi

Dear Diary,

I weigh 126! Yes! I am so excited! Three pounds down and only six more to go. I know I can do it in six days—a pound a day keeps the fat away. This is great! I did the bagel-in-the-toaster-oven trick again, and set the table with my breakfast just as Mom was leaving for work. Then after she left, I poured my juice in the sink and took the bagel in my purse to school.

Today I picked up the script for the play. They want all the girls trying out to read for Alice's part, even if you don't want to play her. That way they're sure to get the best Alice. I know I could never be Alice, but maybe I could get a smaller part, like the Queen of Hearts (at lunch today I kept saying, "Off with her head! Off with her head!"). Monica says I should reach for the top—that's her philosophy, and why not—she's pretty and talented and guaranteed to go far. As for me, well, that's another story.

I wasn't sure what I was going to do about supper tonight, but guess what, dear Diary, when I got home from school there was a note on the table from Mom. It said she had two Mary Kay appointments after work so she wouldn't be home until 7:30 at least, so I should just make myself a frozen dinner in the microwave and eat without her. Oh, Diary, can you believe my good luck? I called Monica right away and she thought it was great. Then she made me say some of Alice's lines over the phone to her and then I did some homework and now I have to go because I just heard Mom come in so I want to go downstairs and say hello to her.

Till tomorrow, dear Diary,

Judi

Dear Diary,

Today I weighed 125 pounds—mazel tov! That means congratulations. When I came downstairs this morning, Mom looked at me for a minute and then she said, "Judi, you look kind of pale, are you feeling okay this morning?" I hope she's not getting suspicious or anything. "I'm fine," I told her. "It's probably because it's almost time for my period." I hope she believed me. I have to be careful so she doesn't find out about Operation Fast. Last night when I came downstairs to say hi to Mom, she handed me my pocketbook which I'd left on the hallway steps and I could see the bagel from yesterday's breakfast stuffed right next to my wallet. I'd completely forgotten to throw it away at school! What if when Mom picked up my shoulder bag, the bagel had fallen out? I guess I could have made up something. I'm getting pretty good at lying, which is a weird thing to say. Mom thinks I had some cottage cheese and fruit for breakfast today because she saw me put some in a bowl before she left for work, but I just dumped it into the toilet as soon as I heard her car pull out of the driveway.

Monica and I ate lunch together as usual, though of course I didn't eat, and she said she really admired the way I'm sticking to my fast. Nancy Pratt ate with Bruce Kaplan, of course—she was practically sitting on his lap! If Paul Weinstein ever did a cartoon of them, I know what he could call it: "Twins Separated at Birth, Making Up for Lost Time." Paul Weinstein ate with Richard Weiss again and this time I sat facing their table and Monica sat across from me. "Is he looking? Is he looking?" she kept imitating me, but I wouldn't look over her head to try to catch Richard Weiss's eye. "Look what I have for lunch: chicken," she said, holding out her sandwich. "Remind you of anyone we know?"

"Very funny." I don't care what Monica thinks. I'm not going to risk looking up and making a fool of myself. When lunch was almost over, I breathed out in Monica's direction to make sure I didn't have bad breath.

"Pee-yew!!" she said, but she was only kidding. The reason I had her check was that my mouth still tastes weird from the fasting, I guess, kind of like how your mouth feels when you first wake up in the morning. I'm chewing gum (sugarless, of course) and I also took two aspirins this morning because my head kind of hurt a little. Other than that, and my stomach growling like a mad dog once in a while, I'm really fine.

I told Mom that me and Monica went to McDonald's again and she said, "What's this with McDonald's all of a sudden?" I just shrugged my shoulders and Mom looked at me. "You still look pale, Judi, you shouldn't be eating all that junk food. A growing girl like you needs fresh fruit and leafy green vegetables, not greasy hamburgers and french fries."

I told her I was sorry and I wouldn't do it again and she said okay, but I'm kind of worried about what I'm going to tell her tomorrow. She came up to my room after the news was over and she stood in my doorway in her work clothes except she was barefoot with her pumps dangling from her left hand.

"Is everything okay, Judi?" she asked, and I could tell she suspected something, but she wasn't sure what.

"I'm just nervous because we're putting on this play, *Alice in Wonderland*, and I'm thinking of trying out."

"Oh, Judi, that's great!" Mom got all excited like I knew she would, which is why I didn't want to tell her in the first place. I mean, what if I don't get a part? Then she'll be really disappointed.

"You know Muriel from my office?" Mom asked. "Her son was in their senior play, *Fiddler on the Roof* last year, and we all went down to see it. They did a really good job, too."

"Mom, calm down. I don't even know if I'll get a part or not." Just what I need—my mom telling her whole office that her daughter is going to be the next Winona Ryder. Well, at least it took her mind off what I'm putting or not putting into my mouth. Mom said she would help me with my costume and then she left and

I could tell she felt better after we talked about the play, so it's good that I told her, I guess. Now it's time for my exercises and then to bed, so good night, dear Diary.

Love,
Judi

Friday, October 7

Dear Diary,

I weighed 124 pounds this morning—yippee!! Gotta go, Mom's calling me. You'd think I'd be tired from all this not eating, but it's just the opposite. Last night I had so much energy, I didn't fall asleep until after 2:00 A.M.! And then I had this weird dream that this huge chocolate ice cream bar with popsicle sticks for arms and legs was walking down the street and then it started to chase me, so I ran as fast as I could and then I looked back and the ice cream bar was melting and underneath the chocolate coating and the ice cream was this really creepy-looking skeleton with brown frizzy hair like me. Weird, huh?

Really gotta go, dear Diary. I'll write more later.

Later

Dear Diary,

I hate Mom. I could absolutely kill her. I mean, I'm going to be fourteen in three months, I'm not a baby anymore. It's none of her business what I eat or don't eat. I swear, she doesn't care one bit. It's like she *wants* me to be the size of Ms. Roth and the fattest girl in the entire eighth grade.

Here's what happened: I got home around 6:00 and I told Mom I'd eaten at Monica's. So she asked me what I had and I said macaroni and cheese. I swear, dear Diary, it's getting so easy to make stuff up, maybe I should be a professional liar if there is such a thing. Anyway, Mom didn't say anything about it, which was a relief, so I went upstairs to do my homework.

A little while later, Mom came upstairs and knocked on my door. I yelled, "Open for business," so she came in and sat down on my bed.

"Judith, what did you have for supper last night?" she asked, and I got nervous because Mom never calls me Judith unless she means it.

I didn't look up from my homework as usual, but Mom said, "Judith, look at me," so I did. She had that up-and-down crease between her eyebrows that she only gets when she's really, really serious, and on top of that, she was sitting on my fluffy pink flowered bedspread in her navy blue business suit so she looked totally, totally stern.

"I had a frozen dinner, like you said I should," I told her, but my heart was beating kind of fast.

"What kind of frozen dinner?" she asked.

"Chicken."

"Oh, really?" Mom got off my bed and started pacing around the room like she was a lawyer on *L.A. Law* or something. "That's funny. I could have sworn I bought two chicken dinners last week and for some reason both of them are still in the freezer. And what's even funnier," she paused and I silently added the words, *Your Honor,* "is that you had macaroni and cheese for dinner tonight, when according to Mrs. Pellegro, the rest of Monica's family had fried fish."

"You called Mrs. Pellegro?" I couldn't believe it. "Did you call McDonald's to check up on me, too?"

Mom just shook her head and asked me what was really going on. I knew she wouldn't understand, but I tried anyway. "Look Mom, I'm sorry I lied to you, but I have to lose weight and the suppers you make are just too fattening."

"Judi, you have a very nice shape—"

"For a hippopotamus!" I interrupted her before she could tell me once again for the millionth time how important it is for a "growing girl" to eat.

"Judi." Mom came over and stood next to me. "You're only thirteen years old. You're too young to go on a diet. You have to eat three balanced meals a day and get all your nutrients. You're going to turn out just fine. All girls your age worry about their figures."

"How come boys don't have figures?" I asked. I'd never really thought about that before.

"I don't know, honey. That's just the way it is. Believe me, you look fine."

Honestly, Diary, sometimes I think my mother is blind. I asked her if I could please join Weight Watchers and she said no and then she went into this whole thing about beauty being only skin deep. "Anyone who's beautiful on the inside is beautiful on the outside, too," she said, "and if you really want to improve your appearance you can start by wearing something other than dark, baggy clothes." She picked up my brown sweater from the floor and tossed it onto my bed. "And put a smile on your face once in a while." I didn't say anything, so then I guess Mom tried to make peace by offering to take me shopping. "There'll be lots of sales for Columbus Day," she said. "Let's go to the mall and see what's doing."

"No, thanks," I said. I'm not going to buy anything new until I weigh 120 pounds, but of course I didn't tell Mom that.

Then I had to go downstairs and eat supper—my first food in five days, and I hate to admit it, dear Diary, but it sure tasted good and I don't even like meat loaf. Mom said from now on I *must* be at the table at 6:00 *sharp* or else. "I don't want to have to worry about you becoming anorexic," Mom said, and I just had to laugh. Me anorexic, dear Diary? Fat chance!

Love,

Judi

Saturday, October 8

Dear Diary,

Me and Monica hung out at the mall today, as usual. There's just nothing else to do in this town. There were lots of great sales, but there's no point in buying any new clothes until I get down to 120 pounds. I weighed 125 this morning, even though I only ate two pieces of meat loaf last night with a salad and a small serving of canned corn. This morning Mom made me eat breakfast. She sat down and drank her coffee while I ate, so there was nothing I could do except eat an entire English muffin—120 calories, probably 150 because I put some butter on it. So much for Operation Fast. I hope Mom calms down soon—she watched me like a hawk the whole time I was eating. I've got to get down to 120 pounds, even if it kills me.

So guess who we saw at the mall today, dear Diary? Richard Weiss! He was with Paul Weinstein, which I still think is weird, a dreamboat like Richard Weiss being friends with a nerd like Paul Weinstein. (God, I hope no one says that about Monica and me being friends, I would just die!) I mean, Mom always says you can't judge a book by its cover, so just because Paul Weinstein isn't the handsomest guy in the world doesn't mean he isn't nice or anything, I guess. Actually, he even has these thick, long eyelashes which can be really pretty, only you can barely see them behind those thick black glasses, and with his nose buried in a comic book like every second.

That's where they were, in the bookstore. Paul Weinstein was standing near the front of the store looking at a comic book, so we peeked in and spotted Richard Weiss behind him. Maybe I should get a job in a bookstore, dear Diary. I wouldn't mind, especially if all my customers were as good-looking as you know who!

Anyway, Monica pulled me by the sweater and said, "C'mon, let's go in and say hello," but I wouldn't budge. She said in a firm voice, "Now, Judi, come on. What if he sees us and we don't say hi? Then he'll think you're ignoring him and that you don't like him at all."

"He wouldn't think that," I said, but Monica could tell I was weakening so she said, "C'mon, I dare you," and she gave me a little push. I started to go in, Diary, but I was so nervous I knocked over a whole shelf of Roseanne Arnold's book, *My Lives*, which were on this sales cart outside the store, and me and Monica ran away laughing hysterically.

God, I hope Richard Weiss didn't see us. He is so cute, I don't know how Monica thinks I could just go up and talk to him. She says, "You'll never know until you try," which of course is easy for her to say. If I was thin maybe I would, but right now I'm such a chunk I could pass as Roseanne's twin. God, if I was as fat as Roseanne Arnold, I'd never star in a TV show, especially since they say the camera adds ten pounds, but Roseanne really doesn't seem to care, which really puzzles me. She even found someone to marry her, so maybe there's hope for me, but I doubt it. The way I look now, no one's ever going to ask me out on a date, let alone for my hand in marriage.

I know if I was thin, Richard Weiss would like me and everything would work out fine. If, if, if—dear Diary, do you think my secret desires will ever come true?

Love,

Judi

75

Dear Diary,

I am so depressed. I weighed 126 pounds this morning. I'm way too fat to try out for the play now, and if Mom keeps making me eat, I'll gain back all the weight I lost and then I really don't know what I'll do. Last night Mom ordered take-out Chinese food, which she knows is my favorite. I didn't have any rice (it was fried). I just had a small portion of chicken with mixed vegetables, but who knows what was in the sauce? It's probably really fattening. Mom got an egg roll for me, too, but I only ate the inside part. When Mom gave me one of her looks, I said, "I can't eat that—it's deep fried and everything and my skin is oily enough as it is." Mom said, "Judi, you have beautiful skin," and sighed one of her sighs, which means she was willing to let it go this time, which was a relief because I didn't have to eat it and we didn't have to talk about my weight and my eating yet again.

Guess what my fortune cookie said, dear Diary? "You will soon realize your dreams." Fat chance, huh Diary? My dream of being the thinnest girl in the entire eighth grade (or the second thinnest, after Nancy Pratt) is going right out the window, along with any hope of ever going out on a date with Richard Weiss. Especially since after supper I had a minor pig out.

Mom went into the living room to watch the 7:00 news (I swear she thinks she would die if she missed it) and I stayed in the kitchen to make her an after-supper cup of coffee (she'd probably die if she missed that, too). So I filled the tea kettle with water and as I was putting it on the stove, I caught my reflection in it (it's one of those shiny metal kinds) and Diary, my face was all weird and wide and flattened out like one of those mirrors in a fun house or something. I just looked really strange. So then I put the water up to boil and got Mom a mug from the cabinet and when I turned around, there was my face again in the toaster, looking like a circus freak. I just couldn't get away from myself except when I opened the refrigerator to get out the half-and-half, and before I knew what I was doing, my hands started untwisting the twistie on the bag of bread and then before I knew it, I was smearing the end piece with chunky peanut butter, and then before you could say, "Mwfh!" which is about all you can say with your mouth full of bread and peanut butter, I was off and eating again.

It's funny, dear Diary, Mom's so worried that I'm not eating enough, and here I am stuffing my face, worried that Mom will find out how much I actually am eating. Only it's not really funny at all. I had a peanut butter and jelly sandwich and a few Oreo cookies and then thank God the water boiled so I could make Mom her coffee and get out of there. I wish I could talk to Mom about all this, but she doesn't really understand. She would just tell me I have a nice figure or I'll grow out of it, or something else that just isn't true. She asked me if I wanted to watch the Sunday-night movie with her, but I said I had too much homework and then I came upstairs and did forty-five sit-ups and forty-five leg lifts. Maybe I should be an aerobics instructor, except of course that's yet one more job you have to be thin to be good at. Oh well. I wish I could just lock myself away from food forever.

Love,
Judi

Dear Diary,

No school today for Columbus Day. I didn't do much of anything, but since I was home and Mom was home, I had to eat breakfast, lunch, and supper. There's no way I'm going to try out for the play now, I'm way too fat to even go to school, let alone to get up on stage in front of an audience. I threw the script out and when Mom came upstairs to say good night, she said, "Break a leg tomorrow," and I almost wish I would. Then I wouldn't be able to walk to the refrigerator and back so many times, eating all this food. I didn't tell Mom I wasn't trying out. I just didn't feel like getting into it with her. It's a stupid play and I probably wouldn't have gotten a part anyway so I don't really care.

I'm going to do my exercises now, dear Diary.

Love,
Judi

Dear Diary,

I still weighed 126 pounds this morning, so there's no way I'm going to embarrass myself by even thinking about being in the play. And besides that, I woke up with the biggest, ugliest, most disgusting zit on my chin that you could possibly imagine. I knew Tommy Aristo would say something about my "headlight" today and of course he did at lunch, but I just ignored him because me and Monica were having a fight.

"What do you mean, you're not trying out?" she asked me between bites of a gooey tuna fish sandwich just dripping with mayonnaise. "I can't believe it, Judi. We've been rehearsing your lines all week."

"I know," I said, popping open my diet Pepsi, "but I've gained back my weight and I just wouldn't be comfortable on stage in front of everyone."

"That's ridiculous," Monica said, tearing open her bag of potato chips. "First of all, you look the same to me as always. Second of all, everyone sees you every day, so they all know what you look like already anyway. And third of all, who cares? Some performers are much bigger than you, and it doesn't matter, as long as they can act. Or sing. You should see some of the opera singers I see on television. They're twice as big as you."

"Oh, thanks a lot." I know Monica was just trying to make me feel better, but for some reason talking to her only made me feel worse. "You know I could never be Alice," I told her. "I probably couldn't even be the

Queen. If anything, they'd pick me to be Tweedledum or Tweedledee. I'm so big, maybe I could even play both of them."

"Oh, Judi, you're being ridiculous," Monica said. "You know what? I think this whole weight thing is just an excuse anyway. I think you're just too scared to try out."

"I am not."

"You are, too."

"Oh, just mind your own business," I said, and we finished the rest of lunch without saying another word. I hate fighting with Monica. I know she's just trying to help, but she doesn't really understand. She's thin, so she has no idea what it's like.

I came straight home after school and when Mom got home, the first thing she asked me was how the tryouts were.

"I didn't try out," I said casually, like it was no big deal.

"What happened?" Mom asked. "I thought you were really looking forward to it."

"I don't know. I probably wouldn't have time to be in a play with all my homework and everything. And besides, none of the cool kids want to be in some stupid play like *Alice In Wonderland*. Only nerds do babyish stuff like that."

Mom just shook her head. "Judi, I'm sure some very nice kids will be in that play. You shouldn't care so much about being in with the in crowd, if that's going to stop you from doing what you really want to do."

"I don't really want to do anything!" I yelled, and ran up to my room. God, why is everyone on my back all of a sudden? If Mom would have just let me fast for a few days, I would have been thin by now and everything would be just fine.

Judi

Wednesday, October 12

Dear Diary,

Well, last night Mom came up to my room and took her usual stance in the doorway and I took my usual place at my desk but then we had a talk and I apologized for yelling at her and everything. "That's all right, Judi," Mom said, coming into my room, "all teenage girls fight with their mothers."

"Did you and Grandma ever fight?" I asked her.

"Did we fight?" Mom rolled her eyes. "Don't ask," she said, in a perfect imitation of my grandmother, and that made me laugh.

"What'd you two fight about?" I asked.

"What didn't we fight about?" Mom shrugged her shoulders. "The way I dressed, the friends I had, the fact that I didn't want to go to shul. . . ."

Wow. It's hard to imagine Mom as a rebellious teenager. She always seems so adult in her work clothes and everything. Anyway, at least she's not mad at me anymore. That's a relief.

And then the absolutely weirdest thing happened after lunch today (by the way, I'm still only pretending to eat breakfast on school days and totally skipping lunch except for diet soda). I went to the girls' room (all this soda makes me pee a lot) and I heard someone getting sick in one of the stalls. "Are you all right?" I asked, but no one answered. I finished what I was doing and came out, but whoever it was was still in there, puking her guts out. I looked under the stall, out of curiosity I guess, and you won't believe who was in there—Nancy Pratt! I recognized her shoes immediately—she's the only girl in eighth grade whose mother lets her wear two-inch heels.

So I said, "Nancy, I'll go get the nurse," and I started to leave, but she yelled, "No, wait, I'm coming out," so I waited to see if she was okay even though I really didn't want to. I mean, she never even says hello to me and if I dropped dead on the street she probably wouldn't even call an ambulance.

Anyway, finally Nancy Pratt came out and she looked really awful. Her eyes were all red and watery and her face was kind of puffy. Still, even like that she looked a hundred times better than I did.

"Are you sick?" I asked, while she washed her face and rinsed out her mouth. "Did you eat something weird?"

She just dried her face and started combing her perfect, straight hair.

"I think you should go see the nurse," I said, while she brushed some blush onto her perfect cheeks. "You look terrible. I mean—" I couldn't believe I had just insulted the most popular girl in the entire eighth grade. "I mean, you don't look well."

"It's nothing," she said, putting some red lipstick on her perfect lips. God, I wish my mother would let me wear makeup. "I just threw up," Nancy Pratt said. "No big deal."

"Maybe you have the flu," I said. Now she was putting mascara on her perfect eyelashes. "I think there's something going around. My mom said two people in her office were out with a bug last week." As soon as I said that, I imagined two people walking down the street with a giant bug between them. Maybe I'll tell Paul Weinstein and he can draw a cartoon of it.

"Judi." Nancy Pratt turned and looked at me. God, she's gorgeous. "I ate too much so I puked. No big deal," she repeated, turning back to the mirror to touch up the eye shadow above her perfect left eye.

I stared at her. "You threw up?" I asked. "On purpose?"

"Yeah. Lots of girls do it, especially models. And actresses and dancers. Where have you been?" She shoved all her makeup back into her pocketbook. "Bruce likes to cut class and sneak over to the cafeteria to eat lunch with me and he hates it when I just sit there and drink ice water while he eats an entire pizza. So I eat, too, and then I get rid of it."

I couldn't stop staring at her. I mean, I've heard of some girls doing that, but no one I knew, and certainly not Nancy Pratt. "But, isn't it disgusting?" I asked.

83

She shrugged. "You get used to it. It's certainly not as disgusting as being fat." She poked my flabby arm. "See ya."

She started walking away, and I could feel the spot on my arm she had just poked stinging. "Wait a minute." I ran after her. "How do you do it?"

"It's easy." She held up two fingers with perfect, manicured nails, red as blood. "You just stick two fingers down your throat and wiggle them around until you gag. No big deal," she said yet again. "Some girls use nail files or something, but you have to be careful. I once read an interview with a model who used a letter opener and ripped her whole throat out."

"Oh my God."

"Relax, Judi." Nancy Pratt laughed. "I'm not going to do anything stupid like that. That girl ruined her entire modeling career. She wanted to be an actress, too."

"Did you try out for the play?" I asked as Nancy Pratt went back to the mirror to check out her perfect reflection one last time.

"*Alice in Wonderland*? That's for babies." She turned and waved at me. "See ya."

"Bye." Thank God I didn't try out for that stupid play, I thought as I watched her leave. God, she has a great figure, Diary, but isn't that the weirdest, strangest, grossest thing you've ever heard?

Love,

Judi

84

Dear Diary,

I'm sorry, I'm sorry, I'm sorry. I skipped writing in you yesterday and now you're not perfect. See, I can't do anything right.

I stayed after class to talk to Ms. Roth about it. Today she was wearing this lime green jumpsuit that made her look like an overgrown grape.

"Ms. Roth," I said, "do you think it's really bad to skip a day in your diary every now and then?"

She looked up from this pile of papers on her desk and brushed the hair out of her eyes. When she did that, these two white plastic bangles she had on raced down her arm and clanged together at her elbow. "Of course not, Judi," she said. "Are you having trouble with your diary?"

"No, Ms. Roth. I just skipped writing in it yesterday. Besides that, I've written in it every single day." I couldn't help but feel a little proud.

"That's great, Judi. That takes a lot of discipline." She put all her papers into her giant leather shoulder bag. "So did something happen yesterday that made you not want to write?"

"Not really," I lied. "I just didn't feel like it."

"I wouldn't worry about it," Ms. Roth said, swinging her bag onto her shoulder. "Just write when you feel like it. The more you let yourself *not* do something, the more you'll allow yourself to do it, too."

I didn't really know what she meant by that, but then

85

the bell rang and we both had to hurry off. I would never tell Ms. Roth the real reason I didn't write in you yesterday, Diary. The reason I didn't write is because I was too depressed. I weighed 128 pounds again and I'm on my way to becoming a Ms. Roth look-alike for sure. Everything was so great the week I fasted and now with Mom making me eat supper every night I just blow it. I tried to talk to her about letting me go on a diet again, but she's just impossible.

"Judi," she said, "food is something to be enjoyed, not something to torture yourself with. Forget all this dieting stuff. C'mon, I'll take you out for some frozen yoghurt."

"Mom!" I just can't believe her. "How can you even suggest that when you know I'm trying to lose weight?"

"Judi, you don't need to lose weight," she said, and I told her to just forget it. Honestly, Diary, I wish I was on a desert island somewhere (as opposed to a dessert island) all by myself with no food and no one to bother me. Of course you could come with me, dear Diary. You're the only one who really understands.

Love,

Judi

Saturday, October 15

Dear Diary,

Today is the anniversary of my dad's death. It's weird, kind of like the opposite of a birthday—a deathday or something. Mom was really sad, but she didn't talk about it much. She said she couldn't believe it was twelve years already since he died and it was getting harder and harder to remember him and that made her even sadder. We lit a Yahrzeit candle for him, which is this special memorial candle that comes in a glass and burns for twenty-four hours. And tomorrow we're going to the cemetery to visit my dad's grave, which is something we do every year. It's near where my uncle Bernie lives, like two hours away.

I tried to be really good and help Mom around the house today without being asked and I even ate breakfast, lunch, and supper without her nagging me. Just for today though, because she's so sad. She even said, "I'm so sorry you never knew your father, Judi," like it was all her fault. So I gave her a big hug and watched TV in the living room with her so she wouldn't be alone (which was good because I couldn't eat anything) but she was still sad. She had these old flannel pajamas on and her ratty terrycloth robe that used to be pink or peach but is now kind of gray. Mom has to be in really bad shape to be downstairs in her PJ's. See, right after my father died she went through this stage of not getting dressed all day unless she had to go out. I was just a baby then and she wasn't working yet, so I guess she spent a lot of days in her nightgown. Anyway, when she snapped out of it, she made a vow that she would get dressed every single morning before she came downstairs and she wouldn't get undressed until she went back upstairs to go to sleep. So I knew she was all upset when I saw her downstairs in her robe.

Sometimes I think Mom is really lonely. I mean, what if by some miracle I married Richard Weiss and then he got killed in a car crash? That would be just awful.

Mom says you can't dwell on the past and the best thing to do is keep busy, which she does with her job and her Mary Kay stuff and everything, but I guess on some days, like today, she just feels all alone. After supper tonight she asked me to make her some hot chocolate instead of coffee and she looked like a little kid, drinking it with both hands holding the mug, all curled up on the couch with her legs tucked up under her. I don't know, Diary, maybe Mom should get married again. She went out on some dates a few years ago but she said they just made her sad and she's not ready yet. Oh well.

Good night, dear Diary,

Judi

Dear Diary,

I'm sorry I didn't write in you yesterday, but I forgot to bring you to Uncle Bernie's house and then we got home really late, so I just went to sleep. I'll write a lot today to make up for it.

Guess what! I met the nicest, cutest, sweetest boy in the whole world yesterday. His name is Michael Silver and he lives next door to Uncle Bernie.

See, yesterday we went to my dad's grave with Uncle Bernie, Aunt Sarah, and my cousin Sheryl, and we said this special prayer and everything and then we all went back to Uncle Bernie's house for some coffee and cake. I said I wanted to stay outside for a while and then I went and sat down on Uncle Bernie's stoop. It was really nice out, "unseasonably warm," according to the weatherman (or weatherperson, as Ms. Roth would probably say). I don't think being a weatherperson would be all that exciting, dear Diary, so that's another occupation we can cross off the list.

Well, of course everyone was all concerned about me. First Mom opened the door and asked me if I wanted to come back inside and I yelled, "In a minute," and then Aunt Sarah tried to get me to come in. I don't know why it was such a big deal. Finally my cousin Sheryl asked me if I wanted to come up to her room and hang out but I just shook my head. Finally Uncle Bernie came out and said to Sheryl, "Honey, I think Judi just wants to be by herself for a while. C'mon back inside." So then they went in and I was left alone in peace.

It's not that I was so terribly sad or anything, Diary. You know the real reason I didn't want to go in: I didn't want to be tempted by Aunt Sarah's famous chocolate-chip-sour-cream coffee cake!

So I was sitting there, and after a while I did start feeling sad about my dad. Uncle Bernie is my dad's brother, and whenever we visit him, I always wonder if that's what my Dad would look like now if he was still alive. They're two years apart (my dad was older) and Uncle Bernie and my cousin Sheryl really love each other. Sheryl's three years older than me and it's not fair that she gets to have a father and I don't. Uncle Bernie and Sheryl do all kinds of stuff together, like go on hikes and do projects in the basement. They built this bird feeder last year and hung it outside the garage and now all these birds come and eat out of it. I bet if my dad was still alive, me and him could make a bird feeder like that, he was really good at making things out of wood. Remember, Diary, I told you he used to do all those carvings? Maybe it runs in the family and I should be a carpenter.

Anyway, I was sitting out there looking at the bird feeder and this little sparrow came to eat from it and I just started feeling sadder and sadder. I guess I was thinking that the sparrow looked awfully little to be out there in the world all by itself and I was wondering why it wasn't safe somewhere in a nest with its mother while its father was out scrounging around for food. Then I decided it was because the sparrow's mother was home in the nest watching all her other kids, and this sparrow had to bring home enough food for the entire family because their father had been killed by some stupid kid with a BB gun and then I really started to cry. I cried for a pretty long time, I guess, and then out of nowhere I heard this voice say, "Are you all right?"

So I looked up and I almost died because there was this dream of a boy standing there with a golden retriever on a leash. I got up immediately and I felt like such a jerk because my eyes were all wet and there was snot dripping out of my nose. Real attractive, huh, Diary? Luckily I had a tissue in my pocket so I wiped my nose and we started talking.

I told him why I was crying (I mean, I told him about

my dad; I skipped the part about the baby sparrow) and then I told him who I was and where I go to school and everything. He told me his name is Michael Silver and he's in the ninth grade and his dog is named Honey because that's what color she is and his mother named her that right before she died.

"Your mother died?" I asked. "How old were you?"

"Seven," he said. "She died of cancer, so she was sick pretty much all the time. But I remember her. I miss her a lot."

"I don't miss my dad," I told him. "I know that sounds weird, but I never knew him, so how can I miss him?"

"That's not weird," Michael Silver said and he looked at me with such a nice look in his eyes that I thought I would die. We talked some more about having only one parent and how hard that is and then he had to go. He lives right next door to Uncle Bernie. They just moved in this past September because his father's company transferred him. That's why I've never seen him before.

Anyway, he's the first kid I ever talked to who had a parent die like me and I felt a lot better after our conversation. Especially because right before he turned to go he said, "It was nice talking to you, Judi." Can you believe it, dear Diary? I was so happy, I didn't eat anything when I went inside Uncle Bernie's house. I hope I get to see Michael Silver again someday.

Love,

Judi

Dear Diary,

I told Monica all about Michael Silver and she was really impressed—a ninth grader! I asked her which she thought sounded better, Judi Weiss or Judi Silver, and she said she liked them both. I asked her who she has a crush on and she said she also had two crushes: Tom Cruise and Patrick Swayze.

"No, really, Monica," I said, "movie stars don't count. You must have a crush on someone."

"I don't really," she said, but then she smiled a little so I knew she was hiding something.

"C'mon, tell me. I tell you everything."

"Oh, all right. My music teacher."

"Mr. Peters? Monica, he's married!"

"I know," Monica said. "That's why I didn't want to tell you."

"But what about someone our age? There must be someone."

"Oh, Judi." Monica rolled her eyes. "All the boys in our class are so immature."

I certainly couldn't argue with that, dear Diary, especially after what happened in English today. Ms. Roth was writing on the blackboard with her back to us and she was wearing this long black sweater and this red wool skirt and part of her skirt was sticking up in the back so you could see her black lace slip underneath. So Tommy Aristo yells out, "Hey, Ms. Roth, are you going to SLIP Ernest HEMingway onto our reading list?" and everyone cracked up and Ms. Roth had no idea why.

So I turned around and said, "Oh Tommy, why don't you just be quiet?" and he said, "What's the matter, Miss Piggy, defending one of your own kind? Oh, excuse me," he rolled his eyes, "I meant *Ms.* Piggy," and then he made all these stupid oinking noises.

So I just turned back around and ignored him, hoping that would be the end of it, but of course it wasn't. At lunch, Tommy Aristo walked by me and Monica's table and pointed to my diet Pepsi and said, "Why, Ms. Piggy, is that all you're having for lunch?" and he oinked away. God, he's obnoxious!

Today I weighed 128 pounds and I'm really fed up. I wish I could just drink Ultra Slim Fast or something, but Mom would never let me. She's still making sure I eat supper every single night. Oh well.

Love,

Judi

Wednesday, October 19

Dear Diary,

This was absolutely, positively, the greatest, most fantastic day of my entire life!

Listen to this: I was sitting in study hall working on this really impossible math problem when this crumpled up piece of paper landed at my feet. I looked up but everyone was studying or pretending to study so I couldn't tell who threw it. So then I picked it up and read it and I almost died.

> Dear Judi, (it said)
> Would you like to go to Tommy Aristo's Halloween party with me a week from this Saturday?
>
> Richard

Can you believe it, dear Diary? Richard Weiss asked me out! It had to be him, there aren't any other Richards in my study hall. I read the note like 85 times while I waited for study hall to be over. It took forever and there was no way I could concentrate on my stupid math problem after that.

So finally the bell rang and I got up and my legs felt all wiggly like J-E-L-L-O, Jell-O! I just couldn't go up to Richard Weiss and say, "I got your note," and bat my eyelashes at him like I'm sure Nancy Pratt would. I mean, what if the whole thing was a joke, like maybe even Tommy Aristo wrote the note and threw it to me and he was just waiting to get a good laugh out of it (at my expense, of course). So I just played it cool and took my time gathering my books together and then Richard Weiss came up to me and asked me if I got his note and I almost died.

Diary, he is so cute I could hardly talk, but I managed to tell him I'd love to go.

"Do you think Monica would want to go with Paul?" he asked.

"Monica and Paul Weinstein?" I tried to picture it. "I don't know. Why?"

"Well," he bent down a little and lowered his voice, like he was telling me this really important secret. "See, Paul has this major crush on Monica, but he's too shy to ask her out, so I told him I'd ask you to ask her, so if she was going to say no, she could without Paul being totally humiliated." He paused, and flipped this straggly piece of hair out of his eye. "He's very sensitive, see, you know, he's an artist and everything, so if Monica said no, he'd be really crushed. And if she says yes, I could tell him and then we could all go together, and that would be a lot easier for Paul."

"Well, I'll ask her," I said, "but I don't know what she'll say."

"Great. Thanks a lot, Judi," Richard Weiss said, and then he put his hand on my shoulder for a second and oh God, Diary, I could hardly stand it. You see how nice Richard Weiss is? (Not to mention sexy.) No other boy would be so concerned about his best friend's feelings. Monica just has to say yes, Diary, she has to. I know Paul Weinstein isn't exactly her type (he's no Tom Cruise or Patrick Swayze, that's for sure) but it would be so much fun to double date. I'd do it for her. I'll let you know what she says, dear Diary.

Love,

Judi

Dear Diary,

Guess what—Monica said yes! I am so happy! When I first asked her she got this funny look on her face, but I begged and begged until she finally said okay.

"I can't believe Richard Weiss asked you out," she kept saying.

"I know, isn't it great? And Paul Weinstein isn't that bad," I added. "I mean, he has a great sense of humor and he's really good at drawing and everything."

"It's okay," Monica said. "It's a good idea to practice going out with a boy you don't really like, in case you do anything dumb or something. Then it's not such a big deal."

Do you think that was a weird thing for Monica to say, Diary? I mean, what if I really embarrass myself in front of Richard Weiss? I'll just die!

I'm going to be really good on my diet starting this very minute. I've got to lose at least five pounds by next Saturday. I wish I could go on a fast again, but there's no way Mom will let me out of eating supper. When I told her I was asked out on a date, she got this goofy smile on her face and said, "Oh, Judi, your very first date! I can't wait to call your grandmother."

"Mom!" I couldn't believe she was making such a big deal out of it. That's what she did when I first got my period, too—called my grandmother right away and I thought I would die.

"Don't tell Grandma yet. Please," I begged her. "I

don't even know if Richard Weiss is my boyfriend or not."

"My little girl has a boyfriend," Mom said, and then she gave me this bone-crushing hug and when she finally let me go and stood back, there were tears in her eyes. Honestly! I only hope it's as big a deal as Mom thinks it is.

Today I was drinking my diet Pepsi for lunch as usual, when Tommy Aristo came up to me and Monica's table and said, "Hey, Ms. Piggy, want to know how to get rid of ten pounds of ugly fat? Cut off your head."

Very funny, huh, Diary? I just ignored him. I mean, who cares about Tommy Aristo anyway? I've got a date—a date with Richard Weiss!

Love,
Judi

Friday, October 21

Dear Diary,

I weighed 127 pounds this morning and I'm going to lose five pounds by next Saturday, even if it kills me. I can't go out on a date with Richard Weiss looking like this. It'll be like Beauty and the Beast, only *he'll* be the Beauty and *I'll* be the Beast!

Last night we had stuffed shells for supper. Mom picked them up already made at this place called Lotsa Pasta. I couldn't believe it—yet another incredibly fattening meal. I didn't know which was better, to take the stuffing out and just eat the shells, or eat the stuffing and leave the shells. Any way you look at it, it's an extremely high-calorie meal.

So I decided to just eat the shells and Mom got really mad and we had another one of our famous food fights. Not the kind where you throw food at each other—though believe me, I felt like it—but the kind where we argue about what I eat.

"Judi, I'm getting really tired of spending good money on food that just winds up going down the disposal. When are you going to get off this dieting kick?" Mom cut into one of her stuffed shells.

"When I'm thin," I answered.

"Judi." Mom put her fork down. "You're a human being. You need food to live. Soon you'll be a woman and women are meant to have curves. We're not sticks, that's all there is to it. Now, eat your supper."

"I'm done," I said, even though there was still lots of food on my plate.

Mom let out this big sigh and said, "Judi, I've had it. I'm sick of going through this every night. You know, you're lucky you have anything to eat at all; there are a lot of people in this world who would give their right arm to have a plate of food like that in front of them. Now you are going to sit there and finish your supper and I don't want to hear another word about it."

"Fine," I said, and I shoved my entire supper into my mouth. Then later after I did all the dishes and made Mom her coffee I just went upstairs into my bathroom and threw up the whole thing. That'll show her. If she's going to make me eat like that, I just don't have a choice. I've simply got to get thin, and that's all there is to it.

It wasn't so bad, dear Diary. I hope you don't think I'm too disgusting. I mean, Nancy Pratt does it, and she says lots of other girls do, too. I did exactly what she told me and I ran the shower so Mom wouldn't hear and then I sprayed some hair spray around afterwards so it wouldn't smell. I mean, Mom hardly ever comes into my bathroom anyway, except when she needs a roll of toilet paper or a tube of toothpaste (we keep the supplies in my bathroom because it's bigger than hers). But I cleaned up real good anyway, just in case. The taste was pretty awful, but I rinsed my mouth out with Listerine.

I guess it's pretty gross and if anyone found out, even Monica, I would die, but I don't really care. I mean, like I said, even Nancy Pratt does it. I'm really relieved because now I know I can eat whatever I want, as long as I have my new "secret weapon."

Love,
Judi

Saturday, October 22

Dear Diary,

Today Monica came over and we planned our Halloween costumes. Monica raided her mother's closet and her brother's closet so we had plenty of stuff to try on.

"How's this?" Monica asked, modeling her brother's football jersey.

99

"You look ridiculous," I said. I mean, it was so big it was practically falling off her.

"Let's see." She put on an old tie-dyed T-shirt of her mother's. "How about this, Judi?"

"I don't know. What are you?"

"A hippie." She put this old chain belt of her mother's around her waist. "Can you believe my mother used to wear this?"

I studied Monica for a minute while she looked at herself in the full-length mirror on the inside of my closet door. "I know. Take your pants off."

"Why?"

"Just try it." Monica stripped. "Now look."

"Wow. You think this looks good?"

"It looks great. It looks like a minidress." I only wish I could look that good.

"You don't think it's too short?"

"No, it looks really sexy. You can wear black tights and I'll braid your hair to frizz it all out and you'll look just like a hippie from the sixties."

"Groovy," Monica said.

"Far out," I answered, and we both giggled. "Now what about me?" We looked around the room which was wall-to-wall clothes on top of the carpet. "And I am not trying on your brother's football uniform." I kicked it with my toe. "I already look like a linebacker as it is."

"Oh, Judi." Monica shook her head. "Let's see what you have in your closet."

"I want to wear all black," I said, moving some hangers around, "so I'll look as thin as possible."

"But what will you be?" Monica thought for a minute. "I know. The Wicked Witch of the West."

"Monica! I don't want to look ugly."

"Well, I didn't mean you had to paint your face green or anything." Monica came out of my closet and started stuffing the clothes she had brought over into two huge shopping bags.

"How are you two doing?" Mom came in and surveyed the mess.

"Well, Monica's all set." I couldn't help pouting. "But I don't know what I'm going to be."

"I'm going as a hippie." Monica modeled her costume. "And Judi wants to wear all black but she doesn't know what to be."

"A funeral director?" Mom asked.

"Very funny."

Mom stroked her chin to think. "You could be a beatnik, Judi. That's what I used to go as every year."

Monica and I looked at each other. "What's a beatnik?"

"It's like a hippie, only beatniks came before, in the fifties. They wore all black clothes, like turtlenecks and berets, and they hung out in jazz joints playing music and reading poetry." Mom held two fingers up to her mouth and pursed her lips like she was inhaling an imaginary cigarette. She snapped her fingers with her other hand and said, "Hey, man, what's happening?" That really cracked me and Monica up. "I think I have an old cigarette holder you can borrow," Mom said. "Without the cigarette, of course."

"Of course." I rolled my eyes at Monica. "What about their hair?"

"Oh, it was mostly long and straight," Mom said, "and hanging in their eyes. Let me see if I can find that cigarette holder for you."

"Hey, man," I said to Monica, "you think you could iron my hair for me?"

"That's a groovy idea," Monica said, so now I'm all set unless it rains and my hair frizzes up, but I guess I can't really worry about that.

Mom made veal cutlets for supper tonight and I ate two without making a fuss or anything. Mom was really pleased. She didn't say anything, but I could tell she was watching the progress of my plate and her face got more and more relaxed as my plate got emptier and emptier. If she only knew what I did afterward! I would die if Mom found out. She'd think it was really disgusting. But after supper she always watches the news, so I don't think she'll ever catch me. Nobody knows my secret except you, dear Diary. Next to Monica, you're my very best friend.

Love,
Judi

Sunday, October 23

Dear Diary,

I weighed 126 pounds this morning. This is too good to be true—I can eat and lose weight at the same time! I'm sure Mom would say something about having my cake and eating it, too, if she knew, but I'm sure not going to tell her.

After supper tonight I went upstairs to do you know what and then later I came downstairs to watch the Sunday-night movie with Mom. She had her feet up on this footstool that my grandmother had embroidered with flowers, and she was rubbing some lotion onto her heels.

"Here, Judi, I have too much on my hand." Mom held out some lotion to me, and I let her smear it onto my palm. "What's that smell?" she asked, wrinkling up her nose.

"I don't smell anything," I said, quickly stepping back from her. I concentrated on rubbing the lotion into my hands and trying not to panic. She couldn't have smelled vomit on my breath, could she? I rinsed my mouth out with Listerine. Twice. I took a sniff cautiously and then I realized what it was. Hair spray. I had sprayed some around the bathroom to cover up the smell and it must have clung to my clothes.

"Oh, you mean the hair spray?" I said casually. "I was trying out a new hairdo."

Mom looked at me. "What'd you do? It doesn't look any different."

I had to think fast. "Well, I tried to put it up in a French twist but it didn't stay, so I just combed it out. Want more coffee?"

"Sure, Judi, I'll take another cup. Thanks."

Whew, that was close! I have to be really careful Mom doesn't figure out what's really going on. She'd probably put a padlock on my bathroom door and then I'd have to get fat again, and you know, Diary, I'd rather die.

Love,
Judi

Dear Diary,

School was really boring today. I can't concentrate on anything except what's going to happen Saturday night. Today Richard Weiss and Paul Weinstein passed me and Monica's lunch table and Richard Weiss said, "Hi, girls," and flipped his hair out of his eyes in that sexy way of his, and I almost choked on my diet soda, he is such a dream. Paul Weinstein said hi, too, and pushed his glasses up his nose with his index finger, which was not sexy in the least. Paul Weinstein just can't hold a candle next to Richard Weiss. It's really sweet of Monica to do this for me; I know she doesn't really want to go out with him. I'll have to think of something special I can do to thank her for it.

I weighed 125½ this morning, which is okay, but I really hope I can make it down to 120 by Saturday. I'm up to fifty sit-ups and fifty leg lifts on each side and I'm only eating one meal a day and throwing up after that. So short of plastic surgery, there's really nothing else I can do to get rid of this ugly fat. At least nobody will ever be able to say I didn't try.

Love,

Judi

Dear Diary,

Four more days until the big date! I am *so* nervous! Richard Weiss hasn't talked to me much, not at all really. I guess he's probably nervous, too. I'm scared we won't have anything to talk about on Saturday. We can always talk about school, I guess. And there'll be other kids there, too. And maybe there'll be dancing, which is really, really scary. I mean, what if a slow song comes on? I would die. Well, at least I know I'll look as good as I possibly can, since black is my most flattering color. I wonder what Richard Weiss is going as. He could go as Mr. America, and he wouldn't even need a costume!

I weighed 125 pounds this morning, dear Diary and I'm glad, but to tell you the truth, I'm not too crazy about this throwing up business. I mean, if anyone ever caught me with my head over a toilet bowl, I would just die. At least it works, though. One thing I wonder is, how does Nancy Pratt kiss Bruce Kaplan after she throws up? They're always kissing on the bus going home after school. I've never kissed a boy and I'm dying to know what it feels like—maybe I'll find out Saturday night! I wish I could ask Nancy Pratt about it, but we haven't really talked much since that day in the bathroom at school. She's in a few of my classes and we say hi sometimes, but that's about it. She is so thin, dear Diary, I'm sure she's going to be a model someday. Who knows, maybe she'll even be on the cover of *Seventeen*! She's got a great body and on top of that, really great clothes (no pun intended!). Today she was wearing the tightest jeans I've ever seen in my life, with little zippers in the back down by her ankles, and she looked absolutely gorgeous. I wish my thighs weren't so lumpy. Oh well. I'm up to fifty-five leg lifts on each side—that should help.

Love,
Judi

Wednesday, October 26

Dear Diary,

I still weighed 125 pounds this morning, so that was kind of depressing. I wish I was thin already. Soon I will be, I guess. Today at lunch, Monica asked me how my diet was going and I told her I've lost like four pounds and she said, "Really? You look the same to me."

"What do you mean?" I asked. "I don't look any thinner?"

"No, not really. I mean, it's not that you look fat," she said, "it's just that I can't see any difference either way."

I don't know, Diary, I guess Monica was saying that to make me feel good, but it didn't really work. She's been acting a little strange lately. Like whenever I try to tell her how nervous I am about my date, she says, "Just be yourself, Judi, and I'm sure it'll be fine." She sounds kind of like my mother, if you want to know the truth. I guess maybe Monica doesn't really want to go out with Paul Weinstein but she doesn't want to say so because then I'll feel bad that I talked her into it. Do you think it was a bad idea, Diary? I'm going to do something really great to thank her for it—you'll see!

Today I had gym, which I absolutely hate, as you know, and we played basketball. We all had to line up and then the two captains picked their teams. I tried to stand in the middle of everyone and blend in, which wasn't too hard to do since we were all wearing the same stupid blue gymsuits. But then the crowd of girls got smaller and smaller, as each girl got picked and ran to stand with her team. I just looked down at the polished wood floor, and kept my eyes riveted on a knot I wished I could disappear into, and waited to hear my name called.

"Pamela."

"Andrea."

"Ellen."

"Judy . . ." I looked up eagerly ". . . Mossman." The captain saw me look up and quickly made it clear it wasn't me she was picking. I looked down again so no one would see my red face, and waited for it all to be over. Finally it was, but my name still hadn't been called. I looked up as I heard everyone else run off to do drills, their basketballs crashing against the floor. Miss Wilson passed me a ball which stung my hands when I caught it, and said, "Just join any team, Judi." Then she ran to the court.

I ran over, too, and started dribbling the ball up and down the gym until Miss Wilson blew her whistle and we all got rid of our basketballs and started the game. No one passed the ball to me of course, so I just ran up and down the basketball court like a zillion times, which is fine with me anyway since it's a great way to burn up calories.

Who cares about gym anyway, right, dear Diary? Only three more days until you know what!

Love,
Judi

Dear Diary,

I weighed 124 pounds this morning. Maybe, just maybe I can lose a pound today and a pound tomorrow and then I'll weigh 122 by Saturday. Wouldn't that be great?

Last night we had chicken for supper and I ate a leg and a wing and a whole baked potato and a salad besides. Mom even made a comment about my "hearty appetite."

"Well, like you said, Mom, I'm a growing girl," I said between bites, "and I have to get all my nutrients." Boy, was I lying through my teeth. I'm glad Mom thinks my dieting days are over, though, and I'm really glad that we don't fight anymore. I hate lying to her, but what can I do?

When we were almost done eating, Mom said out of of the blue, "Judi, what's with these evening showers all of a sudden? I don't want you using up all the hot water at night—we need it for the dishwasher."

"But, Mom." I tried to remain calm. "I get all sweaty from my exercises. I don't want to get into bed all smelly and gross."

"You shouldn't be going to sleep with wet hair anyway, Judi, you'll catch a cold." Mom put her plate in the sink. "And you shouldn't exercise right after supper, either, you could get a cramp."

So now what? I guess I could always run the water in the sink and tell Mom I'm washing out my tights or something if she asks. I mean, I can't exactly say, "Mom, I'm running the water in the bathroom so you won't hear me puking up my food," can I?

Love,

Judi

Friday, October 28

Dear Diary,

I can't wait until tomorrow! Part of me wishes it would hurry up and get here already and part of me hopes it will never come because I am *so nervous*!

Today Richard Weiss waited for me after study hall.

"My father will drive us all over to Tommy's, okay, Judi?" he asked. "We'll pick you and Monica up at 8:00." Then he lowered his voice and leaned down a little and my knees got weak, I swear it. "I wish I could drive us," he said, "but don't worry, my father is cool." What do you think he meant by that, Diary? Do you think he wishes he could drive so he could be alone with me? Oh my God! Then the bell rang and I had to go, which was lucky because my heart was beating so loudly I thought any second Richard Weiss would hear it and think I swallowed a clock like the crocodile in *Peter Pan* that was always after Captain Hook!

And guess what else, dear Diary? I only weighed 123 and a half this morning. My potbelly has definitely flattened out and I'm even beginning to have a real waist.

Love,

Judi

Saturday, October 29

Dear Diary,

Oh my God, it's Saturday! I'm writing in you because it's almost time for me to get picked up (well, there's still an hour to go) and I'm so nervous I don't know what to do! I started getting ready at about 5:00. Mom made me an early supper so I'd have plenty of time to get ready and for once she didn't nag me about my eating because she knew how nervous I was about everything. When I sat down at the table, there was a big ball of tangled yarn at my place.

"What's this?" I asked Mom, "witch's hair? Halloween spaghetti?"

Mom put my supper down in front of me and sat down. She wasn't eating because she was going out later for pizza and a movie with some friends from work.

"This, Judi," Mom said, picking up the yarn, "is something that will take your mind off being nervous."

"How?" I asked, taking a long sip of diet soda.

"See if you can untangle it before your date arrives."

"Fat chance!" I laughed. I mean, this wool was a mess. "How'd you think of that?"

"My mother gave me a tangle of yarn on the night of my first date." Mom got this dreamy look in her eye and started playing with the wool. "I was pacing around the house because I didn't want to sit down and wrinkle my dress and she was sitting on the couch knitting a sweater. Finally she tossed me a ball of yarn and said, 'Here, unknot this for me. You're driving me crazy.' I got so involved in untangling that yarn, I almost forgot I was even going out. When the doorbell rang, I thought, 'Who can that be?' " Mom put the ball of yarn down and looked at me. "And here it is over twenty years later, and now it's your turn."

"Well, thanks, Mom," I said, because I really didn't know what else to say. Then I ate as fast as I could so I could come up here, take a shower, and change. Monica will be over any minute to do my hair and then I'll be as ready as I'll ever be. Wish me luck, dear Diary.

I still weigh 123½, but I don't care. I just know this is going to be absolutely the greatest, most wonderful night of my entire life!

Love,
Judi

Dear Diary,

I hate everyone in the whole world, especially Richard Weiss and even more especially Monica Pellegro, who used to be my best friend and is now my very worst enemy. I am never going back to school again, ever. I am never even going to leave the house again. I am going to stay up in my room and starve to death until I have a completely flat stomach and creamy thighs and amazing cheekbones that look like I'm always sipping through a straw. If I was thin, dear Diary, none of this would ever have happened, I'm sure. I'm so embarrassed, I don't even want to tell you, dear Diary, but you're the only one I can turn to, especially now that I don't even have a best friend.

If you must know, here's what happened: Monica and I were sitting in the living room waiting to be picked up. Believe it or not, I was trying to untangle that stupid ball of yarn Mom gave me and it was calming me down. Until the doorbell rang, that is. My stomach practically turned itself inside out when I opened the door. There was Richard Weiss *on my doorstep* with his father and Paul Weinstein, of course. Mom wanted everyone to come in so she could take our picture, which totally embarrassed me, but luckily everyone was in a hurry to get to the party so there really wasn't time. I just introduced Mom to everybody and then we left.

When we got to the party, everyone took off their coats and showed off their costumes. Richard Weiss was all dressed up like a pirate, in this white shirt with puffy sleeves and a black patch over one eye. Anyone would think he looked really handsome if they didn't know he was such a creep (which I didn't know either, but was soon to find out). Paul Weinstein was wearing a Spiderman costume, except he couldn't wear the mask part on account of his glasses.

Paul Weinstein is really into comic books. He has this huge collection which he says is going to be worth a fortune someday. His father built him these special shelves in his closet because his comic books were really getting out of control, and he has this special notebook that he writes in every time he gets a new comic book, the date he bought it, the title, and a one-paragraph summary of what happens in it. He's hoping Ms. Roth will let it count as his diary, since he writes in it every week. If not, maybe Ms. Roth will let the comic books he draws himself count. He tries to do a drawing every couple of days and he has them in a loose-leaf notebook.

Anyway, I could go on and on and the reason I know so much about Paul Weinstein and his stupid comic book collection is that Richard Weiss didn't say two lousy words to me the whole night. The only reason he asked me out was to get Monica to be his girlfriend. Isn't that the meanest thing you've ever heard, dear Diary? I would never use someone like that. I mean, the thought did cross my mind that maybe I should be friendlier with Paul Weinstein to get close to Richard Weiss, but I'm not a mean enough person to actually *do* a thing like that.

And to think that I've been feeling bad all week about making Monica come on this double date! And on top of that, I was the one to help her pick out a sexy costume. And not only that, I was even going to do something nice for her as a thank-you. I must have been out of my mind. No wonder she's been acting so weird lately, making up that crush on her music teacher, and saying it was better to go out with a boy you didn't really like first for practice. If Monica doesn't really like Richard Weiss, I'd hate to see how she acts with a boy she does like! She spent the whole night talking to him and dancing with him and I just wanted to die. When Richard Weiss went to get himself and Monica some punch, I wanted to go up and say something to her, but Paul Weinstein was talking my ear off, and before I could even say to him, "Listen, I'll be right back," Richard Weiss was handing Monica a glass of punch and practically undressing her with his one patchless eye. Speaking of punch, that's what I felt like doing all right, punching Richard Weiss right in the face so he'd have a real reason to wear an eye patch. Oh, it was awful. I couldn't even call Mom to pick me up because she was still out at the movies. So I just sat there listening to Paul Weinstein go on and on about the Amazing Hulk, which is who I felt like because while I was listening I was stuffing my face with popcorn, pretzels, and potato chips, and I didn't even care.

And that's not even the worst part, dear Diary. Then we played Spin the Bottle and when it was Richard Weiss's turn, he didn't even spin the bottle really, he just kind of moved it until it was pointing right at Monica. And then he kissed her, right in front of everyone! I can't believe Monica reached one of her goals with the boy who was supposed to be *my* date. Monica says she's never kissed a boy before, but she sure looked like she knew what she was doing, let me tell you, even though I could hardly stand to watch. And then later, when we played Seven Minutes in Heaven (don't worry, dear Diary, nobody picked me), Monica and Richard Weiss stayed locked in the bathroom *long* after their seven minutes were up and Tommy Aristo had to bang on the door three times and tell them if they didn't come out soon he was going to have to bust the door down. And then when they came out, Richard Weiss's eye patch was all lopsided and he had this big grin on his face, and Monica's hair was all messed up (the same hair *I* had braided for her) and I just wanted to die. I'm going to have Paul Weinstein draw a really mean cartoon of them and leave it in Monica's locker. I even know what I want him to call it: "Messing Around and All Messed Up."

Anyway, when I *finally* got home, I was so mad, I picked up the ball of yarn Mom had given me and I just threw it across the room. I was so upset, I didn't know what to do. I had dieted and exercised and starved myself to death and thrown up and for what? For absolutely nothing. Oh, I was so mad, I went right over to the refrigerator and ate everything in sight and I mean *everything*. I'm surprised my stomach didn't explode and I wouldn't even have cared if it did. I don't care how fat I get anymore. All that work for nothing, I might as well enjoy *something*, don't you think? At least ice cream, cookies, and bologna sandwiches will never betray me like Monica Pellegro, my *former* best friend.

Love,

Judi

Monday, October 31

Dear Diary,

Happy Halloween, even if it is the worst day of my entire life. I really didn't want to go to school today, but I wasn't up for trying to convince Mom that I was sick. I am sick, though—sick of everything. Sick of being fat, sick of not having a boyfriend, sick of lying to Mom. Yesterday she went to make herself a sandwich and she said, "Judi, have you seen the cold cuts? I thought I bought some corned beef and some bologna on Friday."

"Monica and I had a snack after the party," I said,

116

even though of course you know who ate the whole thing all by herself.

"You girls must have been really hungry," Mom said, taking out the peanut butter, which I had dug into, too.

"Well, um, the boys were here, too," I said, even though I thought she'd get mad to hear that. But she didn't. Instead she asked me the question I knew she was dying to ask me. "How was your date? Did you have a good time?"

"It was all right," I tried to sound nonchalant, "but I don't know if I'm going to go out with Richard Weiss again."

"Why not? He seemed like a nice boy."

Nice boy, ha! If she only knew. "Well, I want to get to know lots of boys before I settle down."

Mom laughed. "I certainly hope so," she said. "You're only thirteen."

Oh, Diary, I am so depressed. Can you see me getting to know lots of boys? Fat chance. It was a really lousy day. I didn't even have anyone to eat lunch with because I certainly wasn't going to sit with Monica. She tried to talk with me on the bus to school this morning, but I just ignored her. We were supposed to go trick-or-treating tonight, but she can just go with that creep Richard Weiss for all I care.

It's probably better that I don't go trick-or-treating anyway, I certainly don't need any candy. Besides, Mom never lets me have the good stuff. Anything that looks homemade, or isn't in its original wrapper, has to be thrown away in case it's full of rat poison or razor blades or something. To tell you the truth, dear Diary, I really wouldn't care.

Love,

Judi

Dear Diary,

Well, I pigged out again last night even though I didn't go trick-or-treating. I stayed home, which surprised Mom. "Trick-or-treating is for babies," I told her, and I just sat at the door handing out candy to whoever came by. The only trouble is, I ate as much as I gave out, or maybe even more. Mom made these little goody bags of miniature Hershey bars and chocolate Kisses and candy corn, and I must have eaten five pounds of chocolate at least.

Don't worry, though, Diary, I got rid of it. My new plan is to get really skinny and have Michael Silver as my boyfriend so Richard Weiss will be really jealous. I haven't figured out how I'm going to get Michael Silver to ask me out yet, but I will. Remember who he is, Diary, that cute boy who lives next door to Uncle Bernie? He's much better looking than that stupid Richard Weiss any day. I don't know how I'm going to do it, but the first thing I have to worry about is getting thin. Then Richard Weiss will see me and Michael Silver together and realize he could have had me and he'll break up with Monica and beg me to please forgive him, but I won't.

I'll never, ever forgive him or Monica either. Monica tried to sit with me on the bus today, but I just put my books down next to me and said, "This seat is reserved." Like Mom would say, "With friends like that, who needs enemies?"

Love,

Judi

Dear Diary,

I weighed 124 this morning, so I guess my Halloween binge didn't do too much damage. My new goal is to weigh 115 by Thanksgiving. We always go to Uncle Bernie's house for Thanksgiving, so maybe I can see Michael Silver again then. I even called information and asked for the number of someone named Silver, living on Toby Lane. "I think it's number fourteen Toby," I said to the operator, since Uncle Bernie's house is number twelve. The operator put it into her computer (God, that's one boring job I know I don't want) and then she said, "No, it's number ten. Here's the number." So now I have Michael Silver's address and phone number! I don't think I have the nerve to call him, but maybe, just maybe I'll write to him. I am kind of lonely, for a boyfriend or even just a friend. I still haven't talked to Monica and even though she's a date stealer and a traitor, I do miss her.

I ate lunch by myself (or rather I *drank* lunch by

myself) today and guess who came over to sit with me? Paul Weinstein. I guess eating with him is better than eating with no one at all. I mean, he is a nice guy, I guess, even though he isn't all that cute. I know looks aren't supposed to be all that important, but I can't help it, they are. Maybe if Paul Weinstein got contact lenses, I would like him better. I know what you're thinking, dear Diary, that that's a really mean thing to say. I mean, how would I feel if Paul Weinstein, or any other boy for that matter, said they'd like me better if I just lost ten pounds? I'm sure that's just what they do say and it hurts my feelings even though I know it's true. Anyway, Paul Weinstein showed me this drawing he had done of everyone in their Halloween costumes. I recognized Monica, and Richard Weiss, and everyone else except this one girl sitting in the corner by herself. "Who's that?" I asked.

Paul Weinstein looked up. "That's you, Judi," he said. "See the cigarette holder?"

"Oh yeah," I said, so he wouldn't think I was insulting his drawing abilities. But Diary, the real reason I didn't recognize myself is that he didn't draw me fat at all. I just looked like anyone else, isn't that strange? "I look like a beat beatnik," I said, and he thought that was pretty clever. "How do you just think of things like that?" he asked, and I said, "I don't know. How do you just draw things like that?" He said he didn't know, it was just something that came easy to him and then he said something really weird.

"I really enjoyed our date, Judi. Maybe you could

come over and look at my comic books and my draw-
ings sometime."

"*Our* date?" I asked, and then I got it. Richard Weiss
must have told Paul Weinstein that he was dating
Monica and Paul Weinstein was dating me! Oh, I got so
mad then, I almost told Paul Weinstein to forget it and
that I was busy every day for the rest of my life and I had
no interest in going over to his stupid house anyway. But
I just said maybe I'd come over sometime because
there's no reason to be mean, just because some people
in the eighth grade are. "What goes around comes
around" is something Mom always says and I hope
Richard Weiss gets what he deserves someday soon.
Mostly, though, I just wish I could close my eyes and
eighth grade would be over.

Love,

Judi

Thursday, November 3

Dear Diary,

I weighed 123½ this morning and I think people are
starting to notice. Paul Weinstein sat with me at lunch
again today. "Here," he said, "I brought an extra comic
book I thought you might like," and he handed me a
Wonder Woman comic. That was pretty nice of him, I
guess. I wish I had super powers like Wonder Woman,
dear Diary. I would fly so far away from here I'd never

have to see anyone again, especially Monica Pellegro and Richard Weiss. They eat lunch together every day now and I swear they're almost as obnoxious as Bruce Kaplan and Nancy Pratt!

Anyway, after a while I was done reading about Wonder Woman, so I put my comic book down and Paul Weinstein put his down, too. "I like your outfit," he said, which was weird because I was only wearing my usual jeans and baggy sweater and no one's ever noticed my clothes before. What I noticed about Paul Weinstein was what he ate for lunch: two whole bologna sandwiches, an apple, a carton of chocolate milk, and three chocolate chip cookies. You'd think someone who ate that much would have something to show for it, but Paul Weinstein is as skinny as a rail. All that eating made it hard for him to carry on a conversation, but I guessed he noticed what I was having for lunch because he asked me about it. "I have a really delicate stomach," I said, which is a joke, "and school food makes me wanna puke" (another joke, dear Diary).

When lunch was over, Nancy Pratt came up to our table and batted her long eyelashes at Paul Weinstein and asked him if she could speak to me in private, which was weird, because really she should have asked me. I couldn't imagine what she wanted to talk to me about, but as soon as Paul Weinstein got up to go, she said, "Sit down, Paul. Judi and I can have a little chat in the girls' room." Then she hooked her arm through mine and we walked down the hall like we were the very best of friends! I wish Monica could have seen us, but she was nowhere in sight. I'm sure she was off somewhere making out with Richard Weiss down by her locker or something.

Anyway, when we got to the bathroom, Nancy Pratt told me some kids had got caught smoking in there last week and now teachers were poking their heads in every two seconds, so would I mind watching the door?

"I didn't know you smoked," I said.

"I don't," Nancy Pratt said. "Smoking makes your teeth all yellow and models have to have perfect teeth. I want you to guard the door so I can . . . you know," and she made this up-and-down movement with her two fingers like she was sticking them down her throat.

"Oh," I said, "of course." Diary, how incredibly stupid can I be?

"I'll only be a minute, Judi. Thanks a lot. I know I can trust you not to tell anyone about this."

"I won't tell," I said, and I went to stand by the door. I tried not to listen while she did it but I couldn't help hearing because the bathroom was pretty quiet. Even the hallway was quiet because fifth period had already started. I just stood there like I was a doorman (or a doorperson) at a really fancy apartment building in New York, which is a job I guess I could handle, even though it wouldn't be too interesting.

Anyway, when Nancy Pratt finally came out, she looked really pale. I wonder if that's what I look like after I do it. She is really skinny, Diary. I bet she has a 19-inch waist just like Scarlett O'Hara from *Gone with the Wind*. She was wearing this black Spandex dress, the kind that totally clings to you, only on Nancy Pratt, there wasn't all that much to cling to.

I watched her "put her face on" as Mom would say, and I asked her if she really thought she was going to be a model.

"I really want to be," she said, brushing some purple eye shadow onto her eyelids, "but the problem is you have to be tall and really skinny. I'm only five foot five, so I hope I grow a few inches. And of course, I still need to lose a little weight. Like there's this one supermodel, Chantelle, she's five foot ten and she only weighs 115 pounds."

"Wow." I couldn't imagine someone six inches taller than me weighing ten pounds less than I do. That's really depressing.

"You can work on losing weight," Nancy Pratt went on, "but there's not much you can do about your height. Or your bone structure. Though you can improve on some things. Like this." Now she was touching up her blush and she turned and swept some makeup over my cheek. "See that, Judi? That makes you look like you have high cheekbones."

I looked in the mirror. "That does look good."

"Let me do the other side."

I turned my other cheek. "My mom won't let me wear makeup until ninth grade." I felt like such a baby telling Nancy Pratt that. You'd think with Mom selling Mary Kay cosmetics and everything she'd understand, but she just says I have beautiful skin and I'm way too young to be clogging up my pores.

"Too bad," Nancy Pratt said. "You have great

eyelashes. A little eyeliner and mascara would really show them off."

I couldn't believe the most popular girl in the entire eighth grade had just given me a compliment. "Oh well," I sighed. "It's just one more year. Then I'll be thinner anyway, and I'll look much better, thanks to you."

"What do you mean, thanks to me?" Nancy Pratt asked.

"You know." I made an up-and-down movement with my two fingers. "This."

"Oh, wow." Nancy Pratt took a step back and looked at me. "Listen, that'll be our signal, okay? We can cover for each other. If anyone else ever found out, I'd be so embarrassed, I'd die."

"I'll cover for you, but I never do it at school," I said as Nancy Pratt went back to combing her hair. "I just skip lunch altogether."

"You're lucky," she said, spritzing some mousse onto her bangs. "I wish I could skip lunch but Bruce hates it when I don't eat. He says it makes him nervous and I'm too skinny. Men!" She shook her hair and started putting all her stuff back in her pocketbook. "Are you and Paul Weinstein going out?" she asked.

"Oh no," I said. "I have a boyfriend named Michael Silver. He's in ninth grade, but he doesn't live around here. He lives near my uncle in Northfield. That's how I met him."

"Maybe we can double date sometime. See ya," Nancy Pratt said, and then she left.

Do you believe it, dear Diary? The most popular girl

125

in the entire eighth grade wants to be friends with me. Who needs Monica Pellegro anyway? And do you believe I told Nancy Pratt that Michael Silver was my boyfriend? I don't know why I said it, Diary, I guess I just wanted to impress her. Anyway, you never know, maybe we will go out someday. I know what you're thinking, Diary—fat chance!—but who knows what's going to happen? Like Mom always says when she watches the 7:00 news, "Truth is stranger than fiction."

Love,

Judi

Dear Diary,

I still weigh 123½ today. I wonder why some days I lose a pound, some days I gain a pound and some days I stay exactly the same.

I started writing Michael Silver a letter today but I didn't get very far. I mean, what if he doesn't even remember me? I could say something like:

Dear Michael,
   Hi, this is Judi, remember me? I'm the
girl you met a few Sundays ago sitting
outside my uncle's house crying, with snot
dripping out of my nose, remember?

Oh my God, I could never send Michael Silver a letter like that, Diary. Sometimes the weirdest things come out of my pen when I write in you. I don't think of them, it's like they just appear out of nowhere.

How about this:

Dear Michael, (take two)
   Hi, this is Judi, remember me? I'm the girl you met a few weeks ago whose father died and we had a short conversation outside my Uncle Bernie's house, remember?
   Well, I was just writing to say hi, and to see how you were doing. I hope everything is going okay. And I just wanted to let you know that it was nice talking to you.
   Give your dog Honey a pat on the head for me.

                                          Judi

How do you think that sounds, Diary? I don't know. "We had a short conversation" sounds kind of formal, and maybe "pet your dog Honey for me" sounds kind of babyish. I don't know if I'm going to really mail it or not. We'll see.

                                          Love,
                                          Judi

                                          Sunday, November 6

Dear Diary,

I didn't write in you yesterday because I had nothing to say. Life's pretty boring when you don't have any

127

friends. I guess I could go to the mall by myself but I wouldn't want to risk bumping into you know who and you know who.

Even Mom, who never notices anything, knew something was up. I knew she was watching me out of the corner of her eye all evening, but she didn't say anything until the Sunday-night movie was over. There was this stupid perfume commercial on that showed this gorgeous guy and this beautiful girl rolling around on some beach and I just couldn't stand it anymore so I grabbed the remote control and just zapped it off.

"Judi, what's the matter?" Mom asked. "You've been kind of quiet all evening."

"Oh, nothing really," I said, but I guess I didn't sound too convincing.

"I'll believe that when the kitchen sinks," Mom said, and I had to smile.

"Well, if you must know, Monica and I had a fight," I said, "but don't even ask me what it was about because I'm not going to tell you." The last thing I wanted to hear was one of Mom's dumb sayings like, "All's fair in love and war," or something. I swear, Mom has an expression for every occasion.

"Can you tell me a little bit of what it was about without going into all the gory details?" Mom asked in a gentle voice.

"Monica did something that hurt my feelings and she won't apologize because she said she didn't do it on purpose to be mean. She thinks I should just forget it, but I can't." I folded my arms over my chest.

"Everyone makes mistakes, Judi. Monica's your best friend. You shouldn't be so hard on her." Mom paused for a minute. "You know what they say: 'To err is human, to forgive is divine.' "

"Why are you taking her side?" I slammed the remote control down on the arm of the couch.

"Judi—"

"Oh, just forget it," I said, and I stomped up to my room. You see what I mean about Mom and her stupid expressions? How can she possibly expect me to forgive Monica for what she's done?

I wonder if Monica and Richard Weiss had a date this weekend. Not that I really care, dear Diary, I'm just curious. More importantly, I wonder if Michael Silver had a date. I rewrote his letter in my best handwriting, put it in an envelope and sealed it, but I still haven't decided if I'm really going to mail it or not.

Gotta go do my exercises, Diary. Now they're more important than ever. I'm up to sixty sit-ups and sixty leg lifts on each side.

Love,

Judi

<u>Monday, November 7</u>

Dear Diary,

Guess what? I only weigh 122 pounds! That's the least I've ever weighed in my whole life (except when I was a baby, of course). My clothes are starting to get big on me, too. I mean, I always wear them baggy to begin with, but now they're really starting to be too big. I'm not going to buy anything new until I weigh 115, though—only seven pounds to go!

You know, I don't care what they teach you about the four food groups. You don't need to eat that much to stay healthy. If everyone ate as little as me and Nancy Pratt, there'd be enough food to go around and so many people wouldn't be starving to death all over the world.

I "covered" for Nancy Pratt today, Diary. She gave me our secret signal in English class so I met her in the girls' room right after. She said Bruce brought her a doughnut and coffee for breakfast before school and she had to eat it. "He ate three doughnuts," she said. "That's like 600 calories. Plus he has sugar *and* cream in his coffee. I swear, if I ate like him, I'd look just like Ms. Roth." She giggled and I did, too, even though I felt a little bad. I mean, I like Ms. Roth.

"How much do you weigh?" I asked. "I mean, if it's not too personal."

"One hundred and five," she said, and I could tell by her voice she was proud. Thank God she didn't ask me how much I weigh, dear Diary. I mean, I'm an inch shorter than she is, and I weigh seventeen pounds more! And to think I was happy with my weight this morning. I don't think I'll ever look like Nancy Pratt, no matter how much I diet. Nancy Pratt isn't big boned like me, but maybe I could get my weight down to 105, or 110 at least.

I just stood there, watching Nancy Pratt comb her hair. I'm always watching her watch herself in the mirror. She caught my eye and asked, "Does your boyfriend make you eat when you go out together?"

For a second I didn't know what she was talking about, but then I remembered. "Oh, Michael," I said. "No, he doesn't really care what I eat."

"You're lucky," Nancy Pratt said. "Bruce is always telling me I'm too skinny and making me eat something. Every day he brings me a snack or a treat. Hey, do you have a picture of Michael? I bet he's cute."

"Um, it's in my locker. I'll show it to you next time," I said, and then I quickly changed the subject. "So do you puke every day?" I asked, and Nancy Pratt nodded. I guess we're going to have to do this every single day for the rest of our lives. Oh well. I guess that's the "price of beauty," like Mom's always telling her customers.

Love,

Judi

<hr />

Tuesday, November 8

Dear Diary,

This morning on the way to the bus stop, I mailed my letter to Michael Silver. I hope he writes back. What if he really does become my boyfriend? I wished that I could be friends with Nancy Pratt and now I am, so maybe that wish will come true, too.

131

Tonight Monica called. Mom answered the phone and she didn't tell me who it was or I never would have taken the call. I said hello and as soon as I heard Monica say, "Hi, Judi," I got really mad. I made my voice really unfriendly and just said, "What do you want?"

She said, "I don't know, just to talk. Want to go to the mall with me this weekend?"

"What's the matter, is Richard Weiss busy?" I asked.

Then Monica's voice got kind of unfriendly. "Listen Judi, I can't help it if he likes me better than he likes you. What do you want me to do, not go out with him?"

That's exactly what I want her to do, but of course I would never say so. So I just said, "I thought best friends were supposed to stick together."

"You're the one who's been avoiding me," she said. "I've been trying to talk to you for over a week. Listen, Richie says it's okay if you hang out with us sometimes. He thinks you're very nice."

Very nice. I almost puked without sticking my fingers down my throat. "What am I supposed to do, sit around and twiddle my thumbs while you two make out?" I asked. "That sounds like a lot of fun."

"Oh, Judi, we wouldn't do that in front of you."

"Why not? You did at Tommy Aristo's party."

"We did not. We just kissed once when he got me in Spin the Bottle."

"Don't remind me," I said, and then my voice shook and I almost started to cry. "I don't know, Monica.

Ever since that stupid party, I feel like I lost my best friend."

"I still want to be your best friend," she said. "You're the one that's pushing me away."

"But you stole my boyfriend!"

"He wasn't your boyfriend, Judi. You didn't even have a real date with him."

"I did, too!"

"You did not, Judi. Richie said he only asked you out because he was too shy to ask me out, so it doesn't really count."

"But," I started to tell Monica about the note Richard Weiss wrote me, but my words got all stuck in my throat. She probably wouldn't have believed me anyway, and I had no way to prove anything since I ripped his note into a million pieces and flushed it down the toilet the night of Tommy Aristo's party, I was so mad.

"So Judi, tell me about *your* boyfriend," Monica interrupted my thoughts. "I hear his name is Michael Silver."

I squeezed the receiver tight. "Who told you that?"

"Nancy Pratt. And I told Richie and he told Paul Weinstein, which is too bad because Paul really likes you and I thought it would be perfect if you started dating him because then all four of us could hang out together. I can't believe you're going out with a ninth grader, Judi. What's he like? Why didn't you tell me?"

"Because it's none of your business," I said, slamming down the receiver. Oh, Diary, what a mess I'm in! Now the whole school thinks I have a boyfriend and I don't.

Even Paul Weinstein would have been better than no one, I guess. Now I don't even have a chance with him. Oh well. Fat girls don't deserve boyfriends anyway.

Love,
Judi

Dear Diary,

I still weigh 122, even though I don't really care anymore. I guess I do care, but I just feel like I don't care. Does that make any sense? I don't know, I thought losing weight would make me happy, but my life is worse than ever. Now I don't have a boyfriend, even though everyone thinks I do, I don't have a best friend, and all my classes are totally boring except English. We just read this really great book called *The Cat Ate My Gymsuit*. It's about a fat girl like me, which of course Tommy Aristo had to point out to the entire class when I handed back everyone's quizzes. I don't know, Diary, do you think I should be an English teacher like Ms. Roth? The only trouble is, I can't imagine spending the rest of my life yelling at obnoxious kids like Tommy Aristo, who can't seem to be quiet for more than two seconds.

Anyway, I wish I could tell Miss Wilson, our gym teacher, that the cat ate my gymsuit. We're playing volleyball now and I can never get the ball back over the net when it comes to me. At least I can serve, though. I make my hand into a tight fist, take a deep breath, and pretend that volleyball is Tommy Aristo's head. Wham! You should see how far over the net I can make that ball go.

Love,
Slugger *Judi*

Thursday, November 10

Dear Diary,

You'll never guess what happened today, dear Diary. Ms. Roth's *husband* came to school! Can you believe it? I guess her car was getting fixed or something so he had to drop his car off for her to use while he got a ride, or maybe his car was getting fixed and he had to borrow hers—I didn't really get the details. Anyway, she was writing on the blackboard when there was this knock on the door and in walks this guy who was absolutely *gorgeous*, like Tom Cruise, Patrick Swayze, and Michael Silver all rolled into one!

Ms. Roth smiled and said, "Class, I'd like you to meet my husband," and everyone's jaws dropped instantly. Nobody could believe it.

"So these are the students you've been telling me about," Mr. Roth said as he made his way up to the front of the room. "They don't look *that* bad." Then he gave Ms. Roth his car key and then, much to everyone's disappointment, including Ms. Roth's, he left. Ms. Roth tried to go on like nothing had happened, but she had this little smile on her face like she was really thrilled that her husband had dropped in so she could show him off.

Don't you think it's strange, dear Diary, that fat Ms. Roth has a dreamboat husband? He really is her husband, Diary, I checked his left hand and his wedding ring was the same as Ms. Roth's, only a little bigger. Either he married her for her money, which I doubt, because if she was rich her clothes would be a lot nicer, or he married her because he felt sorry for her, but why would he do that? He could have anyone he wanted, even someone like Nancy Pratt who caught my eye and shrugged her shoulders like she didn't get it either. Maybe Mr. Roth is one of those guys who thinks that beauty on the inside is more important than beauty on the outside, like Mom's always saying. I mean, Ms. Roth *is* really nice and everything. It's just that she's got some major flaws in the appearance department. There's always the possibility that when they got married Ms. Roth was thin, but that doesn't make any sense either. I mean, why would she want to blow it when she's got this great looking guy? Unless she's got some kind of medical problem and it really isn't even her fault.

Then there's always the possibility that it was a joke, dear Diary. Maybe she hired him to pretend he was her husband for the day. I mean, I'm pretending that Michael Silver is my boyfriend, but I don't think Ms. Roth would go to all that trouble just to impress us. I can't figure it out, dear Diary, but if he really is her husband, maybe, just maybe there's some hope for me, too.

Love,

Judi

Dear Diary,

Another boring weekend to look forward to. I wish Monica would dump Richard Weiss—fat chance of that ever happening though. They hold hands all over the place at school and she sits on his lap at lunch and practically spoon-feeds him his shepherd's pie. Pretty nauseating if you ask me. When I got up to throw my diet Pepsi can away, I had to walk right past their table. Richard Weiss was saying something to Monica and she was looking up at him, batting her eyelashes, but when she saw me walking in their direction, she looked down at her hands like she was really embarrassed or something. Then, once I was past them over by the trash barrel, I turned around and there she was again, laughing up at him like she didn't have a care in the world. Only her laugh sounded kind of loud and fake, if you want my honest opinion.

And speaking of nauseating . . . I'm down to 121 pounds. And I've decided when I get down to 115, I'm going to stop throwing up. I'm just going to eat three small meals a day and I'll only puke if I gain any weight, which I won't. I know I'll never let myself get fat again.

I "covered" for Nancy Pratt again today. This time, while she was doing it, I pretended I was her bodyguard like that movie, *The Bodyguard*, where Kevin Costner has to guard Whitney Houston. I wonder what it would be like to be a famous person's bodyguard. Of course bodyguards are always men so it's not something I could ever really be, which figures because that's one job that sounds like it could be interesting or at least glamorous.

Anyway, Nancy Pratt really looked thin today. She was wearing this V-neck bodysuit and I swear, her collarbones were sticking out like pencils. She said she was really glad she's gotten to know me especially since I'm so trustworthy and everything. "Most kids in this school can't keep their mouths shut about anything," she said. "If anyone ever found out, it would be all over the entire junior high in two seconds flat." I know what she means, dear Diary. Rumors spread faster than peanut butter around here.

I almost asked Nancy Pratt if she wanted to hang out with me this weekend, but I couldn't get up the nerve. I mean, why would a thin, beautiful, popular girl like that want to hang out with a fat social outcast like me? And besides, what if she suggested that the four of us go out—her and Bruce Kaplan and me and Michael Silver? Then I'd really be in a pickle.

Maybe Michael Silver will write back to me, Diary. I mailed the letter on Tuesday, so he probably got it on Wednesday. So if he wrote back on Thursday, that means I should have gotten a letter back from him today, which I didn't. Of course, maybe he isn't going to write back right away, maybe he's going to wait a few days. But if he really liked me, wouldn't he write back the very same day he got the letter? I know I would. But boys are different. Oh well. I know a cartoon Paul Weinstein could do of me sitting by the mailbox. He could call it, "Waiting for Mail from a Male." But even Paul Weinstein doesn't sit with me at lunch anymore. I guess he feels rejected. I don't really like him "that way" if you know what I mean, dear Diary, but it would have been okay for us to have been friends, I guess. Now I have nobody, dear Diary. Nobody but you.

Love,
Judi

Saturday, November 12

Dear Diary,

No letter from Michael today. I asked Mom if we were going to Uncle Bernie's house for Thanksgiving and she said of course, since we go every year. It's only two weeks away and I still have six pounds to lose. See, even if I don't hear from Michael Silver, I figure I can go next door to his house and just say I came over to wish him a happy Thanksgiving. What will probably happen is, he won't recognize me and I'll tell him who I am and he'll say, "You're kidding. You can't possibly be the same girl. She was so fat and you're so thin." Then he'll say, "I'm so glad you came by. I've been meaning to write to you, but I haven't had time." And then he'll ask me out. Oh, Diary, wouldn't that be great?

I ate a small bowl of cereal for breakfast today and half a sandwich for lunch. Whatever Mom's making for supper won't be a problem. Down it goes and up it comes. Sometimes I wish I could just dump my plate right into the toilet instead of having to eat and throw up. It pretty much amounts to the same thing.

Love,

Judi

Sunday, November 13

Dear Diary,

Well, no mail today, so I couldn't be disappointed about not getting a letter from Michael Silver. "There's always tomorrow," as Mom likes to say.

I was really kind of cold today and even with my heaviest sweater on, I felt kind of chilled. Of course Mom noticed I was wearing a heavy sweater in the house. "Are you cold, Judi?" she asked. "A little," I said, so she went to check the thermostat, though I don't know why. She always keeps it on 68 degrees during the day and 58 degrees at night because our house is heated with oil which is expensive.

"I hope you're not catching a cold," Mom said. "Maybe I'll make some matzo ball soup." Mom smacked her lips but I didn't respond. I really hope she doesn't make soup, dear Diary, because you'll never guess what the secret ingredient is: chicken fat! It's supposed to be like Jewish penicillin or something.

Then Mom said I looked kind of pale, so I ate a big supper so she wouldn't be suspicious. Thank God she made tomato soup instead of chicken soup; it's much less fattening though I don't know what the difference is. It all comes up anyway.

Winter is definitely in the air. The leaves are all gone from the trees and the branches all look like skinny arms with bony fingers reaching up toward the sky.

Love,

Judi

Monday, November 14

Dear Diary,

Today Nancy Pratt gave me the signal, so I met her in the bathroom and she was in there for a really long time. When she came out, she asked me if I ever have any blood in my puke, and I told her no, and she said that she did sometimes.

"Maybe you should stop," I said, watching her weave her hair into a French braid. "You look really great."

"I still have this, though," she said, patting her rear end. "The famous Pratt ass. A present from my mother, thank you very much."

Diary, if Nancy Pratt has a fat ass, what does mine

look like, a tank? "How much do you weigh now?" I asked her, and then I had to wait because she had a bobby pin in her mouth.

"One hundred and three," she said, pinning up a loose strand of hair. "I'm trying to get down to a hundred pounds, but those last three pounds are really hard to lose."

"I don't know, Nancy," I said as she put on her lipstick. "I mean, what if you bleed to death? I think you should stop and just go on a diet, like Weight Watchers or something."

"No way," she said. "One thousand calories a day would be a disaster for me. My metabolism's so slow, I can gain weight just from watching Bruce eat."

"I know what you mean," I said. "I can gain weight just from thinking about food." We both laughed. I don't know, Diary, maybe we really will become friends after all. At least Nancy Pratt is too concerned with herself to ask me about my boyfriend. That's a relief. No letter from Michael Silver today. Oh well.

Love,
Judi

<u>Tuesday, November 15</u>

Dear Diary,

Today was a great day! First of all, I weigh 120— hooray! I am so happy! The sweet taste of success (no

142

pun intended). I wore a blouse tucked into my jeans today instead of a baggy sweater for the first time ever and I got lots of compliments. Tommy Aristo winked at me and Nancy Pratt said I looked really good even though my outfit would be improved by a belt, which of course I was too dumb to even think of.

I told Mom I wanted to go shopping for new clothes and she said maybe I could get some for Chanukah. Chanukah starts on December 9th and I'm sure I'll be even thinner by then. Mom doesn't seem to notice, though. I mean, I am still pretty heavy, and the first couple of pounds are just water weight, but still, you'd think she would notice that her only daughter is finally starting to look halfway decent. All she cares about is that I eat my supper (I eat it all right, but I don't digest it).

Now that my weight is getting under control, I really want to start wearing makeup. That day Nancy Pratt put blush on my face, I looked really good. So I decided to ask Mom about it after supper when she was relaxing in front of the TV. I brought in her coffee, sat down on the couch next to her, and waited for a commercial to come on.

"Mom," I said, "can't I start wearing makeup now? I don't see why I have to wait until ninth grade."

"Judi, we've talked about this before. You're too young to be putting powder all over your face."

"Please?"

She took a sip of coffee. "The answer is no."

"Pretty please?"

"No."

"Pretty, pretty please?" I jumped off the couch, got down on my knees, and begged with my hands clasped to my chest. "Pretty, pretty, *pretty* please?"

Mom looked at me and shook her head, but she couldn't hide the smile on her face. "We'll see, okay?"

"Okay." I got up just as the news came back on. "We'll see" isn't exactly yes, but it isn't exactly no, either, Diary. I guess that's progress.

Well, that's it, dear Diary. I'm still more than ten pounds fatter than Nancy Pratt, but at least I'm losing my chipmunk cheeks and my waistline looks pretty good. I still have a potbelly and ridiculous thighs, though. Think Mom would let me get liposuction, dear Diary? Fat chance!

Love,
Judi

Wednesday, November 16

Dear Diary,

Today a really weird thing happened. Paul Weinstein was giving his oral report in English and I kind of blacked out, I think. He was doing it on *Catcher in the Rye* which we had to read last year, so I don't know how he's going to get into Harvard if he keeps cheating like that. He doesn't really want to go to college, he wants to go to art school, but his father will never go for that.

Anyway, one minute he was talking about the beginning of the book when Holden Caulfield is at this football game and then I kind of went away somewhere because the next thing I knew, I looked up and there was Paul Weinstein with his mouth moving up and down and his glasses slipping down his face like his nose was some kind of crazy waterslide and then I shook my head and realized he was talking about the part when Holden Caulfield sneaks into his parents' house and wakes up his little sister Phoebe, which is at the end of the book, and class was practically over and I hadn't heard a word Paul Weinstein had said. And it wasn't like I was daydreaming or anything, it was like I had sort of disappeared.

Weird, huh, Diary? Anyway, I'm back and luckily Ms. Roth didn't notice anything.

Love,
Judi

Thursday, November 17

Dear Diary,

Guess what, guess what??!! I got a letter from Michael Silver! He wrote back, can you believe it? Here's what he said:

> Dear Judi,
>   I got your letter a couple of days ago, on my Mom's birthday in fact, isn't that a

coincidence? I was pretty sad the whole day at school, so it was nice to come home to your letter.

I'm pretty busy with school and after school I have football practice and then I have homework of course. And I do the dishes after supper because it's just me and my dad and to tell you the truth, he's not the world's greatest cook. My Mom was a really good cook though. Sometimes my father tries to cook something she used to make, like meat loaf, but it never comes out the same.

Thanks for writing,
Michael

What do you think about that, Diary? It's not exactly a love letter, but he did say it was nice to get my letter. And he did write back. I'm going to write to him again soon.

Now I just have to get down to 110 pounds by Thanksgiving. Ten pounds to go—I know I can do it. It'll be hard not to eat a lot at Uncle Bernie's because Aunt Sarah really puts out a feast and everyone just eats and eats and tells her how good it all is. Last year I read about this family in Massachusetts who fast on Thanksgiving because of what happened to the Indians. I mean, the Indians showed the Pilgrims how to grow corn and everything and then the Pilgrims turned around and killed them. That's what the mother of this family said anyway. I wish I could go to their house for Thanksgiving but Mom would never let me. And anyway, if I don't go to Uncle Bernie's, I won't get to see Michael Silver. I wonder if I should write and tell him I'll see him on Thanksgiving, or just surprise him. I can't decide, so I guess I'll "sleep on it."

Love,

Judi

Friday, November 18

Dear Diary,

The absolutely most awful thing happened in school today. It was really, really scary and it was even partly my fault.

Here's what happened: Nancy Pratt was in the bathroom throwing up and I was standing at the sink running the water in case anyone came in. She was in there for an awfully long time, so finally I knocked on the door and said, "Nancy, are you all right?" but she didn't answer.

I knocked a couple more times and then I got kind of scared so I just crawled underneath the door, and oh my God, Diary, Nancy Pratt had collapsed right over the toilet!

God, it was awful. There was puke in her hair and everything. I tried to get her up but she was really out of it and then I got really, really scared so I ran to get someone as fast as I could. The first person I saw was Ms. Roth coming out of the faculty lounge.

"Ms. Roth," I said, "come quick. Nancy Pratt is sick." Ms. Roth took one look at Nancy Pratt and told me to go get the nurse right away and then the nurse came and she told Ms. Roth to go call an ambulance and then the ambulance came and took Nancy Pratt away.

I really couldn't concentrate on my schoolwork after that and I felt pretty shaky when I got home. Mom was still at work and I really wished there was someone around I could talk to. I almost called Monica but instead, dear Diary, I opened the refrigerator and started eating and I ate and ate until I really felt sick.

I didn't want to throw up because I was scared I would pass out like Nancy Pratt, but I had to, Diary, or else I would have *burst*. And the weird thing is, as soon as I did it, I wanted to eat again, so I had a few cookies and a glass of milk and then I wanted to puke again. So I was on my way upstairs, but luckily Mom came home so I went back down and said hi to her and acted like everything was normal.

After supper I puked again and I sprayed Lysol around the bathroom to hide the smell. Just as I was finishing, I heard Mom come upstairs and go into her bathroom. A minute later she knocked on the door. "Judi, can I come in? I need a roll of toilet paper."

"Just a minute," I said, wishing we didn't have to keep the extra supplies in my bathroom. I sprayed a little more Lysol around and made sure the toilet seat was clean. Then I brushed my teeth and opened the door. "Here, Mom," I said, handing her a roll.

"I like your hair up like that," Mom said. I had put it up on top of my head with a barrette so I wouldn't get any puke in it if I passed out, like Nancy Pratt did. That was really gross. "It looks very flattering up away from your face like that. What are you doing, cleaning?"

"Yeah," I said, since the bathroom really stunk of Lysol. God, that was close. I better be careful, dear Diary. And I really am worried about Nancy Pratt. Do you think I should have told someone about the blood in her barf? Maybe if I had, she wouldn't have passed out and none of this would have happened. And now I'm scared that someday I'll pass out, too. My stomach is really in a knot, dear Diary, and for once it's not just from all this food.

Love,

Judi

Saturday, November 19

Dear Diary,

No word about Nancy Pratt yet. I called the hospital and they said she's in intensive care and can't have any visitors.

As soon as I hung up the phone, Monica called and before I even had a chance to make my voice unfriendly she gave me the news: she and Richard Weiss broke up. I couldn't believe it. "What happened?"

"He went out with Diane Adams last night."

149

"Diane Adams?" I was shocked. "But she's a ninth grader!"

"I know," Monica said. "And get this: *she* asked *him* out."

"Wow! He told you that?"

"Well, not right away. We were supposed to go for a walk this afternoon and he showed up an hour late, so we had a BIG fight about that. So then he wanted to kiss and make up, so he takes his jacket off, and . . ." Monica paused for dramatic effect, ". . . he had this gigantic *hickey* on the side of his neck."

"Gross!"

"You're telling me. So that's when he told me all about his date last night. So we had another fight and I said I was too young to be cheated on and he said he was too young to be tied down and so then we just broke up."

"Wow." I didn't know what to say. Part of me wanted to say, *that's great*! because I'm glad Monica's not going out with Richard Weiss anymore, and part of me wanted to say *I'm really sorry, Monica*, because what he did must have really hurt her feelings. I mean, I have no idea what being cheated on feels like, since I haven't had a boyfriend yet, but it's gotta feel pretty lousy, don't you think, dear Diary?

Then Monica asked, "How's your boyfriend, Judi?" and for a minute I didn't know what she was talking about. But then I remembered.

"Oh, he's okay, I guess," I said. "I don't really get to see him very much, so we're sort of like pen pals." I'll probably see him when we go to Uncle Bernie's for Thanksgiving, so it was sort of the truth.

"From what Nancy Pratt said, it sounded like you two are really an item."

"When did you talk to Nancy Pratt?"

"One day in homeroom. Why, do you own her or something?"

"No," I said, "but I didn't know you were friends with her."

"I'm not," Monica said stiffly. "But since you wouldn't talk to me anymore, I just kind of asked her about you, since you two seem to be hanging out."

Was Monica jealous that I was friends with Nancy Pratt? "We don't hang out that much, Monica."

"I thought she was your new best friend."

The other end of the phone got really quiet while Monica waited for me to say something. This was my chance to get back at her and say something mean, like, "No, I used to have a best friend, but I don't anymore," but when I opened my mouth, my chin started shaking like I might cry. "She's not my best friend, Monica," I said. "You are. If you still want to be."

"Judi, I'm really sorry I went out with Richard Weiss. I do want to be best friends again."

"But are you sorry because he turned out to be a two-timing creep, or are you sorry because you hurt my feelings?"

"Well, both, if you want to know the truth." Monica let out a big sigh. "I mean, he is cute, Judi, you have to admit. I never told you I had a crush on him, because

151

you did, too, and then at Tommy Aristo's party, I couldn't resist. But now I know even a date with Tom Cruise wouldn't be worth it if it meant losing my best friend. I've missed you a lot."

"I missed you, too," I said, and then I did start to cry and I could hear Monica crying, too, and then we both cracked up. I'm really glad we're best friends again. Monica asked me if I wanted to go to the mall with her tomorrow and of course I said yes. She said she had a music lesson in the morning but she would be done by 1:00 and then we could go.

So that's that. I wish I could tell Monica all about Nancy Pratt, and what really happened, but Nancy Pratt would kill me, I'm sure. Oh well. I'm glad me and Monica are all made up.

Love,

Judi

Sunday, November 20

Dear Diary,

Today Monica and I went to the mall and I'm really glad we're best friends again. We went into our favorite store, Clothes-R-Us, and just out of curiosity, I tried on a pair of 9/10 jeans, and guess what? They fit!

"Wow, you look really great," Monica said when I came out of the dressing room. "You should wear tight jeans more often, Judi. They look really good." That sure was music to my ears, dear Diary. I bought two pairs of jeans, one regular and one black.

"I really admire your willpower, Judi," Monica said. Oh God, if she only knew the truth. If it wasn't for the "beauty tip" Nancy Pratt taught me, I'd be fat as a pig. I can't imagine telling anyone about it though, not even Monica.

See, ever since Friday, dear Diary, I've been eating nonstop. I'm too scared to weigh myself—I'm sure I put on a pound or two. And I really think I should stop puking. I mean, besides being really gross, I guess it's kind of dangerous. But I can't stop doing it until I stop pigging out and this weekend was a real disaster.

At least I told Monica all about Michael Silver, Diary. I told her we never really went out and I showed her the letter he wrote me (I carry it in my pocketbook all the time). We decided I should write back and let him know I'm going to my uncle Bernie's house so I'll see him on Thanksgiving.

We went into this stationery store where they sell paper by the pound because Monica said I shouldn't just write it on notebook paper. "How about this?" she asked, pulling down a pink sheet of paper.

"No," I said. "That's too girly. Nothing pink and nothing with hearts."

"What about this, then?" Monica took a piece of gray paper down from a shelf.

"Bor-ing!"

"I was only kidding. That's résumé paper." Monica put it back. "You pick something, then."

"Maybe a card would be better," I said, so we went over to look at them. Couples strolling on the beach was too obvious, and flowers in a vase was too formal. Finally I found a card that had a golden retriever pictured on the front of it that looked just like Michael Silver's dog, Honey.

We went to sit down at a snack bar to write the letter. While Monica ate some french fries, I drank a diet soda and wrote out what I wanted to say on a napkin. After about ten false starts, this is what I came up with:

> Dear Michael,
> Thanks for writing back. I know what you mean about being sad on your mother's birthday. My dad's birthday is April 26th and even though I never knew him, like I told you, I still feel pretty sad and my mom feels really sad the whole day.
> I am going to visit my uncle Bernie for Thanksgiving so maybe I'll visit you, too. It would be nice to see you again.

I printed it out on the card in my best handwriting and showed it to Monica.

"That's good," she said. "How are you going to sign it? 'Love, Judi'?" She handed the card back to me.

"Of course not!" I snatched the card and put it down on the table carefully so it wouldn't get any soda or ketchup stains on it. "That's too obvious."

"You could spell it L-U-V," Monica suggested, tracing the letters in the air with a red-tipped french fry.

"N-O."

"What then?" Monica popped the french fry into her mouth. "Very truly yours?"

"I'm just putting my name," I said, writing it down.

"Put a little heart over the *i* instead of a dot."

"Monica!" I put the card in the envelope and addressed it. "Do you have a stamp?"

"No, let's go to the post office." Monica started to get up and then stopped. "Oh, it's closed on Sunday. Too bad. We could have gotten a Love stamp."

"Will you stop with the love?" I finished my soda with a slurp.

"Boy, are you touchy. I was only teasing." Monica started to clear off our table. "C'mon, there's a stamp machine in the drugstore."

We went to the drugstore and I got a plain stamp with an American flag on it. I'm going to mail Michael Silver's card tomorrow and then he'll get it on Tuesday or Wednesday, so even if he wanted to write back, he wouldn't have time to.

That's it for now, dear Diary. There's school tomorrow, so I better do my homework. At least there's one good thing about school days—it's a lot easier to stick to my diet.

Love,

Judi

155

Dear Diary,

Well, I guess I'm sort of a hero because I kind of saved Nancy Pratt's life. Maybe I should be an EMT or something. That stands for emergency medical technician, but I don't really think I could be one, since I can't stand the sight of blood. Paul Weinstein even gave me a cartoon he drew. It had two parts: one was of me kneeling down next to Nancy Pratt and the other was of a big submarine sandwich and the caption was "Two Heroes," get it? I thanked him and said, "See, you can think up captions on your own when you want to," and he said, "Yeah, but they're really not as good as yours." Then I said to him, "You know, you can still eat lunch with me sometimes, if you want to," and he looked down at his feet and mumbled something about having to go and then he just ran off.

Anyway, Nancy Pratt is out of intensive care, but she's still in the hospital. I don't think anyone knows what's really wrong with her but me. Tommy Aristo asked me if she was preggo, which just shows how much he knows.

Ms. Roth asked me to stay after English for a minute today. After everyone was gone, she came out from behind her desk so she was standing right next to me. She was wearing this flower-print dress which wasn't too unflattering since it had a navy blue background and she had some kind of flowery-smelling perfume on too.

"So, Judi," she said in a soft voice, "what exactly

happened in the bathroom the other day?" Ms. Roth looked straight at me, but her voice was more, I don't know, concerned than mad. She seems like she really cares and that almost made me cry for some reason.

"I don't know, Ms. Roth. I guess Nancy Pratt just fainted." I couldn't look Ms. Roth in the eye because I was afraid if I did, she'd see I was lying and I just couldn't give away Nancy Pratt's secret. Or my own for that matter.

"Do you know why there was so much water on the floor?" Ms. Roth asked, her voice still soft.

I had to think fast. I was running the water to drown out the sound of Nancy Pratt's gagging, and in all the excitement I forgot to turn it off, I guess, but of course I couldn't say that. "I was washing my hands when I heard this thunk and then I found Nancy Pratt and I was so worried about her, I guess I forgot to turn off the water."

"You had good reason to worry," Ms. Roth said, and then she sighed. "Nancy is a very sick girl." She waited but I didn't say anything. "Judi." Ms. Roth took a step toward me and then stopped. I could feel her looking at me, even though I kept my eyes on the tip of one of her navy blue pumps. "Are you sure there's nothing else you want to tell me? Nancy is in serious condition, so any information you have about what happened that day would be really helpful."

The tip of Ms. Roth's shoe blurred. I swallowed hard and just shook my head.

Ms. Roth sighed again. "All right, Judi," she said, like

157

she was giving up. "But if you think of anything, you can always come talk to me." Then she let me go. I don't know, Diary, maybe I should tell her, but if I do, Nancy Pratt will kill me. Oh, why does life seem so complicated all of a sudden?

Love,

Judi

Tuesday, November 22

Dear Diary,

Today when I called the hospital they said Nancy Pratt could finally have visitors, so I walked over there to see her. The hospital was really kind of creepy. It smelled sort of like the school cafeteria for one thing, and then there were all these nurses walking around with clipboards and carts of medicine, or wheeling someone in a wheelchair. I didn't like it at all, so forget about me ever getting a job in a hospital.

I went up to the fifth floor and found Nancy Pratt's room. A nurse was just coming out so I asked her if I could go in and visit. The nurse said Nancy didn't want to see anyone from school, so I said, "Just tell her Judi Liebowitz said hi," and Nancy Pratt must have heard me because she called out to the nurse that I could come in.

I could understand why Nancy Pratt didn't want anyone from school to see her, dear Diary. She looked awful. She had these huge black circles under her eyes and she was as white as this piece of paper I'm writing on. Even saying hi to me seemed to make her tired. I asked her how she was feeling and she said terrible.

"They're feeding me glucose," she whispered, pointing at this tube running into her arm. "And they say I have to eat, and the food is awful, Judi. All starch. They make me eat three meals a day and if I don't eat, I'm not allowed to watch TV. And," she gripped my hand, "they're not letting me out of here until I gain seven pounds."

"Oh my God. Seven pounds?" I stared at her. "Then you'll weigh 110."

"I know," she moaned, "I'm much too short to carry all that weight." She was quiet for a minute and I looked away because she was starting to cry. "Judi, you've got to help me figure something out. I'll die if I gain seven pounds."

To tell you the truth, dear Diary, Nancy Pratt looked like she would die if she *didn't* gain seven pounds. She looked just like a skeleton lying there, but of course I didn't tell her that.

"Maybe you should just gain enough weight so they let you out of here," I said to her. "You can always lose it again after that."

"I don't know," she said. "I can't stand the thought of being fat. And if I gain weight and lose it again, I'll get stretch marks." She let out a deep sigh. "They're so mean to me here, Judi. They keep the bathroom locked and when I have to go, I have to call a nurse to let me in. And she makes me leave the door open a crack so she can listen—isn't that gross? I'll just die if I don't get out of here soon."

She clutched my hand again and I'll tell you something, Diary, for someone who looks so weak, Nancy Pratt is really strong. I didn't know what to say to her, but luckily the nurse came in just then. "Visiting time is up," she announced, walking briskly into the room. The nurse was young-looking and for a minute I wasn't even sure if she was a nurse or not because she wasn't wearing a cap or a uniform like the nurses on TV. She was just wearing white pants with a pink blouse and a white sweater, and she even had long dangling earrings on—two in one ear and one in the other. The only reason I knew she was a nurse was that she had a stethoscope hanging around her neck.

The nurse must have seen me staring at her because she smiled and said, "I'll be back in one minute and I want you to be gone," but she didn't say it mean or anything and then she left the room.

"She seems nice," I said to Nancy Pratt, but she just rolled her eyes.

"Judi, will you visit me again, soon?"

"Uh, yeah, sure." I didn't know if I really wanted to, but what could I say?

"Promise?"

"Promise." I guess Nancy Pratt is really lonely, so it's the least I can do.

"Skedaddle." The nurse was back so then I had to go.

Isn't it all horrible, dear Diary? I swear, I'm never going to throw up again.

Love,

Judi

Dear Diary,

Today we only had half a day of school on account of Thanksgiving. I won't be able to visit Nancy Pratt until the weekend, I guess, but maybe by then she'll be home. I kind of doubt she can gain seven pounds by Saturday, but maybe she'll trick them by putting weights in her shoes or something.

If anyone's going to gain seven pounds by Saturday, it's someone with the initials JBL. In other words, *me*. I can't seem to stop eating these days and I'm too scared to vomit. I'll kill myself if I blow up into a blimp again. My new jeans are already getting tight and I only bought them a few days ago! I'm definitely going to weigh myself tomorrow and "face the music." I hope I've only gained a pound, or two at the most. Fat chance, with all the eating I've been doing. If I don't weigh less than 125, I'll never have the nerve to knock on Michael Silver's door tomorrow, even though I'm dying to see him. I hope I don't really blow it at Uncle Bernie's tomorrow, but I'm nervous because Aunt Sarah is such a great cook. I bet she could even be a chef in a restaurant if she wanted, which is one job I wouldn't take even if it paid a million dollars. I guess I could never be a waitress either, for that matter. Being around food all day would be a disaster for me. Oh well. Two more jobs to scratch off the list.

Love,

Judi

Dear Diary,

Happy Thanksgiving! We're getting ready to go, so I can't write much. I weigh 123, so I'm definitely going to see Michael Silver. I'm really excited. I'm going to wear my new black jeans, and Monica is coming over to iron my hair. I'll tell you all about everything tomorrow, dear Diary.

Love,
Judi

Dear Diary,

Thanksgiving was one big fat, and I mean FAT disappointment. When we pulled up to Uncle Bernie's house, the first thing I noticed was there were no lights on next door at Michael Silver's house and no car in the driveway so I knew he wasn't home. And when we went inside, Uncle Bernie gave me an envelope and said it was from "the boy next door." I pretended I didn't really care and that I had to go to the bathroom. As soon as I locked the door behind me, I tore open the envelope and read the note inside. This is what it said:

> Dear Judi,
>   I won't be home on Thanksgiving because first my dad and I are going to eat dinner

with some friends of his from work, and then I'm going to my girlfriend's house for dessert.

See ya,
Michael

Isn't that awful, dear Diary? Michael Silver has a girlfriend! And he didn't even say, "Thanks for writing," this time, or "Write back soon," or anything. I feel like such an idiot for even thinking there was a tiny chance that he might like me. I felt so awful and on top of that I had to "put on a happy face" and go downstairs and eat with my family.

When I came down, Aunt Sarah hugged me and kissed me and said I looked very skinny and gorgeous and then my cousin Sheryl made a big fuss over me, too. They're used to seeing me in baggy sweaters, not jeans and a tucked-in blouse, so I guess my weight loss was really noticeable to them. You'd think I'd like all the attention, but I didn't, really. All I could think of was, they wouldn't say I was so gorgeous if they ever saw me leaning my head over a toilet bowl. And when Aunt Sarah said, "You must have some willpower," I felt like a big fat fake.

And then I ate like a pig because, well, I don't know why exactly. I mean, everyone else was eating away and it tasted really good and Michael Silver had given me the brush-off, so it didn't really seem to matter.

So I just had to throw up when we got home, Diary. I know I said I wouldn't do it anymore, but I really didn't have a choice. I mean, I ate like 5,000 extra calories at least, and we got home pretty late and the worst thing you can do is go to sleep on a full stomach, everyone knows that.

So, I did it. I thought I was safe because Mom had already gone to bed, but when I came out she was standing in the hallway in her peachy pink-grayish robe.

"Are you all right?" she asked.

"I don't feel so good," I said, which was actually the truth. "I threw up a little, Mom. I think it's 'cause I ate too much."

"C'mon, let me put you to bed," Mom said, and she tucked me in like I was a little kid again, which felt kind of nice. "Now, if you feel sick again, you can come wake me up, Judi, okay?" Mom kissed my forehead. "If you feel like you have to throw up again, just call me and I'll help you."

"Okay," I said, even though part of me wanted to laugh out loud at the thought of Mom helping me barf. Then I just went to sleep.

When I came downstairs this morning, Mom was sitting at the kitchen table, but she jumped up when she saw me. "Are you feeling better, Judi? How's your stomach?"

"I'm fine," I said, and then I decided to take advantage of the situation. "Well, I feel a little better, but my stomach's still kind of shaky."

"You better eat lightly today," Mom said, which of course was fine with me. She made me some dry toast and poured me a glass of ginger ale which she stirred around with a knife first to take all the fizz out.

"This should settle your stomach," she said, sitting down across from me. "Remember when you were little and you got sick, I used to let you watch TV in my bed? And I used to bring you toast and ginger ale and you used to insist upon stirring out the bubbles all by yourself?"

I didn't really remember that, but I nodded because it's one of those holidays when my mom gets all sentimental on account of missing my dad, so she likes to reminisce about the good old days. She took a big sip of her coffee and then just sat there kind of quietly while I ate, and I felt a little weird about the way she was just sitting there, looking at me.

"What's the matter?" I finally asked her, and she just sighed this deep sigh. "Judi," she said in this sad voice, "I don't feel like I know you anymore."

"Sure you know me," I said, trying to sound cheerful. "I'm Judith Beth Liebowitz, remember? The kid you're always saying is too young to wear makeup."

But Mom didn't smile. "Judi, you're so quiet lately. You're always up in your room and I never even see you. I didn't even notice that you've lost some weight and I had no idea you were friends with the boy next door to Uncle Bernie."

"He's not my friend," I said, "and I don't want to talk about it."

Mom shook her head. "That's what I mean, Judi. You won't talk to me about anything." I could feel her looking at me, but I kept my eyes focused on the toast crumbs on my plate. "Hey, remember when you were in second grade and that boy stole your hat while you were waiting for the bus and threw it up in a tree? What was his name?"

Boy, Mom was really into strolling down memory lane this morning. I hadn't thought about that in years. I looked up. "Mark Shapiro. He moved away in fifth grade."

"Oh, that's right, the Shapiros." Mom traced her finger around the rim of her coffee cup. "And remember you were afraid to tell me what had happened because you were scared you'd get in trouble for losing your hat?" She looked at me and this time I didn't look away. "But I knew something was wrong and then when you finally told me, we went out with sticks to try and get your hat down from the tree, remember?"

"And by then it was frozen," I said.

"Right." Mom laughed. "And you were sad because you thought your hat would be lonely all by itself up in that tree all winter, so I made up a story about a family of birds that decided to use your hat as a nest and then you felt better?"

"The Birdowitz family." I smiled, remembering. "Mrs. Birdowitz, Mr. Birdowitz, Bonnie Birdowitz, and Benny Birdowitz. They had nowhere to live for the winter, but then they found my hat and they lived in it happily ever after." This time I sighed. I wish it could be that easy.

"I know life isn't that simple anymore, Judi," Mom said, as if she was reading my mind, "and I know all teenage girls keep secrets from their mothers." I must have looked surprised because Mom laughed. "Judi, do you think I was born thirty-eight years old? I was a teenager once, believe it or not. I know it can be rough and I want you to know I'm here for you and if you have any problems, you can always talk to me about them. Even if I don't understand what you're going through, I'm always here to help you and I'll always try to do the best I can. Okay?"

"Okay," I said, and then I went upstairs to take a shower. Do you think Mom suspects anything, dear Diary? I wish I could tell her, but this is much more serious than losing a hat. I don't think I've been acting all that different lately. And besides, it doesn't matter since I'm never going to puke again.

Then in the afternoon, Mom took out her Mary Kay stuff and gave me a facial. That was kind of fun and I know it made Mom feel better. She even showed me how to put on some blush and she said maybe, just maybe I wouldn't have to wait until ninth grade to wear makeup, but she didn't want me bugging her about it.

I guess I should be really happy about that, but I'm not. I mean, I am but I'm still really upset about this whole Nancy Pratt thing and I wish I could tell Mom but I don't know, it's like I wouldn't even know where to start. I mean, if I told her about Nancy Pratt, I'd have to tell her about me, and then what? I don't think Mom would put me in the hospital, but she would know how disgusting I was and I don't think I could take that right now. Just dealing with Nancy Pratt at the moment is enough.

Love,

Judi

Dear Diary,

I went to visit Nancy Pratt today. She's still at the hospital and she looks a little better, but not much. Now they're making her drink these special high-calorie milk shakes, but of course she's not drinking them. She said the first time they brought her one, she accidentally on purpose spilled it all over the bed and the nurse got really mad because she had to change the sheets and everything. Bruce Kaplan was visiting and he drank the second one they brought when the nurse wasn't looking.

Today Nancy Pratt asked me to drink her milk shake but I didn't want to. "C'mon, Judi," she said. "You can go home and throw it up and I can't."

"I'm scared I'll get in trouble," I whispered, because just then a nurse walked by the room.

"No one will know," she said. "Listen, Judi, you wouldn't want me to tell all the kids at school that you puke your guts out and that's how you lost weight, would you?"

I stared at her. "You wouldn't," I said, but I knew she would. "I'll tell on you, too," I said, but she just laughed.

"You think anyone would believe you? Everyone thinks I'm in here because I have an ulcer. Even Bruce. C'mon, Judi." She pushed the milk shake toward me and spoke in a nicer voice. "I thought of all people, you would understand. That's why you're the only one allowed to visit me besides my parents and Bruce. I thought you and I were really becoming good friends."

"I can't, Nancy," I said, hardly daring to look at her. "I mean, I would, but the thing is, I've stopped throwing up, so I just can't."

"Oh, so that's why you look fatter than the last time I saw you," she said, and her voice sounded really mean. Do you think she could really tell, Diary, or do you think she just wanted to hurt my feelings because I wouldn't drink her stupid milk shake? I've only gained three pounds and I didn't think they were that noticeable.

Anyway, luckily Nancy Pratt had a meeting with a counselor then, so I had to leave. She made me promise I would visit her again and I didn't really want to, but I said I would. I guess I feel a little sorry for Nancy Pratt, even though I don't really like her very much. I wish I had a counselor to talk to, or just somebody who would understand, but who? Not Mom. Maybe Monica, but I don't know, it's such an embarrassing problem to have. I'll just have to figure out what to do all by myself. That's what being grown up is all about, I guess.

Love,
Judi

Dear Diary,

I weigh 123½ pounds today. My body is so weird—I'm always losing or gaining weight, but never staying the same. I'm afraid I'm going to gain back all the weight I lost and then everyone will be disappointed in me. Like what will Monica say about my willpower then?

Monica had to practice today because she has a big holiday recital coming up in December and she has a solo and everything. So I didn't do much today except eat, of course. I had a drippy tuna fish sandwich for lunch and Mom said she didn't feel like cooking so we had pizza for dinner and I had three gigantic pieces, and then I just had to puke after that. I know I promised you I wouldn't, dear Diary, but I just can't get fat again. Everyone will laugh at me, especially Nancy Pratt.

What a life, huh, Diary? I bet you wish you belonged to somebody else.

Love,
Judi

<u>Monday, November 28</u>

Dear Diary,

We had this special assembly at school today. A counselor came to talk to us about eating disorders, I guess on account of Nancy Pratt and everything. I don't know if the other kids know, but I guess Nancy Pratt's mother had to tell her teachers something since she's missed so much school.

Anyway, the counselor was about Mom's age and of course she was thin. Well, she wasn't really skinny like Nancy Pratt or anything, but she wasn't fat, either. She

170

was just right, so I didn't think she really knew anything about eating disorders, but what she had to say was pretty interesting. Her name was Miss Fiorino and she was really pretty, in a Dolly Parton kind of way—you know, teased hair (brown though, not blond), lots of makeup, and long red nails.

First she wanted to show us some slides, but of course there was a problem with the slide projector, so while Miss Fiorino was waiting for them to fix it, she took a little survey. "How many of you have ever been on a diet?" she asked. Of course no one raised their hand. "Very interesting," Miss Fiorino said. "I see I have a very unusual group here." She folded her arms across her chest. "Okay, here's another question: How many of you are completely satisfied with the way you look?" Again no one raised their hand.

"Well." Miss Fiorino walked up and down the front of the auditorium, pondering this. "No one likes their body, but no one's doing anything about it. Does that make any sense to you?" she asked a girl in the front row.

"No, I guess not," the girl said.

"So, somebody's lying," Miss Fiorino said, but not in a mean way. "I think we have some members of the Secret Dieting Club in this auditorium." She started walking up and down again and I was scared she was going to pick girls out of the audience whom she thought were on diets, but thank God she didn't do that.

"The Secret Dieting Club is made up of girls aged twelve to eighteen. Most of them are of average weight,

171

but all of them think they're fat. In fact, many teenage girls are dying to be thin, and I do mean dying."

Just then the slide projector was ready, so Miss Fiorino showed us her slides. The first one was of a starving teenager in Africa and the second one was of an American anorexic teenager, and not only did both of them look exactly the same, like their arms and legs were made of sticks and their ribs were just about to poke right out of their skin, but both of them looked just like Nancy Pratt!

Then Miss Fiorino talked about anorexia nervosa and bulimia, or "the binge-purge syndrome" as she called it. Boy, am I glad I don't do that anymore! Last night was the last time, I swear it. Miss Fiorino said bulimia is really dangerous. You can rip the lining of your throat or rot the enamel off your teeth or get ulcers or even stomach cancer. "We are not cows," Miss Fiorino said, showing a slide of some cows grazing in a field. "Cows have three stomachs, but we only have one. Once the lining of your stomach disintegrates, that's it. You don't get a second chance."

Then a boy in seventh grade wearing a Yankees baseball cap asked why anyone would do something dumb like stick their fingers down their throat. Miss Fiorino stopped her slide show and said, "Can anyone answer that question? Why would a girl—because usually it is a girl—do something potentially harmful to herself in order to lose weight?"

"Because it's important to be thin," a girl in the back said, but I couldn't turn around fast enough to see who it was.

"Why?" Miss Fiorino asked.

"Because no one wants to be friends with you if you're fat."

"And boys won't ask you out."

"And you can't find cool clothes to wear."

"And kids tease you at the beach."

"Even your own mother gets mad at you."

"And no one picks you to be on their basketball team." I surprised myself by yelling out along with everyone else.

Suddenly everyone was talking at once and Miss Fiorino had to shout at us to be quiet. "It seems that some members of the audience—some *female* members—have experienced the enormous pressure our society puts on us to be thin."

"Guys feel a lot of pressure, too," a boy yelled.

"Yeah, but if a guy is big, he can be a football player, but if a girl is big, she can't be anything," a girl yelled back.

"I'm not saying you boys have it easy," Miss Fiorino said, "but there is definitely more pressure on females than on males to have the perfect body. Sometimes a girl will develop an eating disorder just because one of her friends or a parent or a doctor or even a stranger on the street makes some comment about her body. That comment, even if it was said with good intentions, like 'You're really pretty, but you'd be a knockout if you lost five pounds,' can make a girl feel pretty bad about herself. And a common response to feeling bad is dieting. And a common effect of dieting is developing an eating disorder."

Then we went back to Miss Fiorino's slide show. It was kind of like a beauty show through the ages. First she showed us these paintings that Rembrandt did, of women who were considered beautiful back when he was alive. All the women were soft, round, and *fat*. Maybe I was just born in the wrong century, dear Diary. Then the slide show jumped ahead to the 1960s and showed this picture of Twiggy, who was a very popular model then. She looked like a stick figure.

"Even Marilyn Monroe would be considered too fat by today's impossible beauty standards," Miss Fiorino said, and it's true. In the slide she showed us, Marilyn Monroe was *really* curvy, especially compared with the next slide of Kate Moss, this supermodel of the nineties. Kate Moss is five feet seven inches tall and weighs only one hundred pounds, and she's the model who started the "waif look," which Miss Fiorino says is one giant step backwards for womankind.

So then Miss Fiorino finished her talk by saying again how dangerous dieting is and that it doesn't work anyway because your body actually slows down its metabolism to adjust to receiving less food. So that's why, when you first go on a diet you lose weight, but then it gets harder for the weight to come off so you start eating even less and then you get frustrated so you binge, and then you get even more frustrated so you try to diet again and before you know it you have a full-blown eating disorder.

"Dieting leads to Frustration." Miss Fiorino drew a map on the board, as if Dieting and Frustration were two cities halfway across the country from each other. "And Frustration leads to Bingeing." She drew Bingeing way on the other side of the blackboard. "Bingeing leads back to Frustration." She walked back to the middle of the blackboard. "And Frustration leads back to Dieting." Now she walked back to the other side of the blackboard. "Dieting leads to Frustration which leads to Bingeing which leads to Frustration which leads to Dieting which leads to Frustration. . . ." As Miss Fiorino spoke, she ran back and forth faster and faster, drawing circles between Dieting, Frustration, and Bingeing, until she stopped, completely exhausted.

"And that's exactly what it feels like to be in the throes of an eating disorder," she said, panting to catch her breath. "So I'm glad no one raised their hand today when I asked if anyone was on a diet," Miss Fiorino concluded, "because I would hate to see anyone in this room suffering like that."

No one said anything for a minute and then a girl from my social studies class raised her hand. "Is there a cure for eating disorders? I mean, once you have one do you have it for life, or can you get better?"

"That's a very good question," Miss Fiorino said. "People with eating disorders can get well. It usually takes a long time and it usually involves going to a support group or seeing a counselor. Remember, it's not a sign of weakness to ask for help, it's a sign of strength." And then her talk was over.

So after almost everyone had left, I went up to Miss Fiorino while she was packing up her slides and stuff, and I told her I had a friend who used to have the "binge-purge syndrome" but she got better all by herself and what did she think about that?

"How long has she been well?" Miss Fiorino asked.

"Oh, a little while," I said, looking down at the floor. I mean, I couldn't exactly tell her I'd only stopped this morning.

"Well," Miss Fiorino said, "it's too bad *your friend* wasn't at the assembly this morning, because I've never met anyone who got better all by herself. *Your friend* would probably have a lot to teach all of us. Without help and a lot of support, even people with a lot of recovery behind them often fall back into old patterns when the going gets rough. So *your friend* must be a very special person." From the way Miss Fiorino kept saying "*your friend*" I don't think I fooled her one bit.

"What should I tell her?" I asked.

"Tell *your friend*," she emphasized the words again and looked right at me with eyes as green as a cat's. I wondered if they were real or if she was wearing tinted contact lenses. "Tell her that you care about her and you want to help her. See if you can get her to talk to someone she trusts, like one of her parents, or one of her teachers at school."

"But what if she doesn't want to tell?"

"Then you might have to," Miss Fiorino said. "Let your friend know that you know what's going on." She snapped her briefcase shut and I was surprised she didn't get her long red nails caught in it. "Girls who are bulimic can be very sneaky and clever, and lots of times

176

even the people they live with don't know what's going on. Sometimes a girl is actually very relieved to know that someone is on to her, and she doesn't have to deal with this all alone. Let your friend know that you care about her and that you want to help her."

"What if she doesn't want any help?"

Miss Fiorino stopped gathering up her things and looked at me again. "What's your name?"

"Judi."

"Listen, Judi." She looked me in the eye and this time I couldn't look away. "Nobody likes a tattletale, but sometimes, even though it might feel like you're hurting your friend, you might actually be helping her. If she's not going to go to an adult for help, you might have to do it for her. If your friend's life was in danger, don't you think telling an adult would be the right thing to do?"

"Uh, yeah, I guess so," I said, and I could feel my eyes filling up with tears.

"I work at a clinic," Miss Fiorino said, handing me a business card. "If you can't do anything else, at least give my card to your friend. Maybe she'll call."

"Thanks." I grabbed the card and got out of there as fast as I could. I wasn't even sure if I was talking about myself or Nancy Pratt anymore. I mean, I don't feel like my life is in danger or anything. And I guess I should have told someone that Nancy Pratt was seeing blood in her vomit, but now she's in the hospital so even if her life is in danger there's doctors and nurses there to take care of her. And I'm never going to puke again. I'm going to have two small meals a day—just breakfast and dinner—and go back to doing my exercises. And I'm not going to lie to Mom anymore, either.

Maybe I can turn my life around, dear Diary, and get back on track. Maybe I should be a counselor like Miss Fiorino, and help girls like me and Nancy Pratt not get into trouble. I don't know, though. I guess for now I better just worry about myself.

Love,
Judi

Tuesday, November 29

Dear Diary,

Everyone was talking about the assembly today and more than a few people were talking about Nancy Pratt. I guess the "cat's out of the bag," as Mom would say. Even Monica brought it up at lunch. She was fooling around with her hot dog, holding it out to the side of her mouth and pretending to play it like a flute. Then she turned it the right way and started eating it. "What'd you think of the assembly, Judi? Can you imagine sticking your finger down your throat? That is so disgusting."

I didn't say anything for a minute while Monica kept eating. Then, after she finished her hot dog and was opening up her milk carton, I said real quietly, "Yeah, I can imagine it."

"What?!" Monica knocked over her milk but luckily

she had been trying to open the carton on the wrong side so it didn't spill. "Judi, what are you talking about?" Her eyes grew wide. "You never did that, did you?"

" 'Never say never,' as my mom likes to say." I tried to be flip but it didn't work. "I don't do it anymore, Monica, and I only did it a few times." I couldn't tell her everything. "You know how much I want to be thin. I thought maybe it wouldn't be too gross, but it was, so I stopped. It was mostly when we weren't talking to each other so that's why I didn't tell you."

"Oh, wow." Monica finally got her milk carton open and took a long sip. "Oh my God, Judi, I can't believe it. What if you had to go to the hospital like Nancy Pratt?"

"I won't. Don't worry. I just skip lunch and that seems to help me control my weight." It's true, Diary. I haven't puked since Sunday and I'm done with all that, I swear it.

"But what if you do it again?" Monica asked. "Remember that counselor at the assembly said you can't get better all by yourself."

"Well you can, and I'm not going to do it anymore."

"Promise me," Monica said. She was really upset.

"I promise."

"Swear it."

"I swear it."

"Shake on it." She held out her hand and we shook.

"God, Monica, why are you so upset about it?"

"Why am I so upset?" She was practically shrieking. "Because I care about you, you nincompoop!"

"Oh," was all I could say. "Well, you have to promise

179

not to tell anyone about it," I said, and Monica promised, swore, and shook on it.

And get this—Tommy Aristo came up to me in study hall and said he needed to talk to me. "Uh, Judi," he stammered, "I just want you to know that, well, I don't know, I tease you and everything, but I don't really think you're all that fat, and I, uh, well, I guess I'm sorry if I ever hurt your feelings."

Then he just stood there, like he was waiting for me to punish him or dismiss him or something. And guess what, dear Diary? Here was my chance to be really mean or something, and I don't know, I just didn't feel like it. So I said, "Hey, Tommy, my mom says, 'to err is human and to forgive is divine.'"

"I don't know if I'd call you divine," Tommy said, but I glared at him and he apologized. "I didn't mean that. I promise I won't tease you anymore." Then he stuck out his hand and said, "Friends?"

"Friends," I said, and we shook on it.

It was quite a day, dear Diary. And not only that, but we had our first snowfall of the year today. It started right in the middle of English. Tommy Aristo said, "God's dandruff sure is heavy today," and pointed to the windows. Everyone turned to look and some kids started getting out of their seats. But instead of yelling at us like any other teacher would, Ms. Roth said, "What are you all waiting for?" Then she made a beeline for the windows, so everyone else did, too, and while we watched the big, fat flakes falling, Ms. Roth recited her favorite poem to us, "Stopping by Woods on a Snowy Evening," by Robert Frost.

Isn't that funny, dear Diary, how you can say big, fat flakes and it doesn't mean anything bad like when you say big, fat person? Maybe in my next life I'll be a fluffy snowflake, the bigger the better!

Love,

Judi

Wednesday, November 30

Dear Diary,

Today Monica asked me to come over after school, but I told her I had to go visit Nancy Pratt. Monica said it was very noble of me to go and I said that I just felt kind of sorry for her. Which is true, I do feel sorry for Nancy Pratt, but the reason I visit her is because I'm afraid if I don't show up she'll tell everyone I used to binge and purge just like her. I wonder if she knows that the whole school knows the real reason she's in the hospital. Well, I'm certainly not going to be the one to tell her.

Anyway, I was feeling a little nervous on my way over to the hospital. I gained another pound so now I weigh 124, and I'm sure Nancy Pratt will notice and say something. I haven't thrown up since Sunday like I promised, but I haven't been good on my diet, either. I know Miss Fiorino said diets are dangerous, but I'm not really dieting, Diary, I'm just watching what I eat. If I didn't do at least that much, I'd really be a mess. As it is, I almost had something for lunch today, but I just filled up on diet Pepsi instead.

181

Nancy Pratt is about the same, I guess. She says she's gained a pound and a half, but she sure doesn't look it.

"Check out my stomach," she said and she lifted up her hospital gown. "Isn't this disgusting?" She pinched a miniscule amount of flesh between her fingers.

It was disgusting, dear Diary, but not because she was fat. She was so thin, her belly caved in like a teaspoon and I could see all her ribs sticking out. Of course I didn't tell her she looked awful. I told her she was still the thinnest girl in the entire eighth grade, in the entire junior high in fact, and then I tried to tell her about Miss Fiorino and everything she said, but Nancy Pratt just shook her head.

"Spare me," she said. "My counselor gives me the same rap. And she makes me do these stupid mental exercises, visualizations, she calls them." Nancy made her voice thin and whiny, imitating her counselor, I guess. "Imagine yourself at a party. You're very thin. Then you get fatter and fatter. What happens now?' " Nancy made her voice normal again. "I'll tell you what happens. When I'm thin, I'm dancing with Bruce and having a great time, and when I'm fat I'm sitting in a corner all by myself and Tommy Aristo is calling me Nancy Fat instead of Nancy Pratt and I'm miserable." She shrugged her tiny, bony shoulders. "So big deal."

"Do you think they're going to let you out of here soon?" I asked her.

"I don't know." She looked around her hospital room and made a face like she was totally disgusted with it. "At least my mother talked to all my teachers so I won't flunk out of school or anything. What I'd like to do is get out of here right before Christmas vacation so I'd have two weeks to lose the weight they made me gain before I had to face everyone at school again."

"But Nancy, you can't lose any more weight. What if you pass out again?" I got this funny feeling in my stomach. "What if you die?"

"Don't be stupid, Judi. I'm not going to die. That was just an accident, what happened in school. I'm not going to pass out again."

I just shook my head and left soon after that and then stopped at the candy store and binged all the way home.

Love,

Judi

Thursday, December 1

Dear Diary,

Only two more weeks and one more day until Christmas vacation. That'll be a relief. I could really use a break. This hasn't been the greatest semester of my life, I guess. I haven't really been able to concentrate on my schoolwork with everything that's happened.

I have so much work to do I don't know how I'll get it done in time, so I'm not going to write so much today, dear Diary. We have a huge math test tomorrow and if I fail it, that'll be just one more problem to deal with. As Mom would say, "I need that like a hole in the head."

Love,
Judi

Dear Diary,

"TGIF," as Mom would say, which stands for Thank God It's Friday.

This has been a rough week. Tons of schoolwork, plus visiting Nancy Pratt at the hospital, and on top of that, eating, eating, eating. I just can't seem to stop, dear Diary, and I hate to tell you this, but I weigh 125 pounds. Isn't that gross? I'm back to wearing my baggy jeans and sweaters again. I'd rather die than be seen in a tucked-in blouse now.

I'm really depressed. Monica asked me why I was in such a lousy mood at lunch and I said it was because I had so much schoolwork to do. She said I was lucky I only had schoolwork, not schoolwork *and* practicing besides. Her recital is at the end of December, right before Christmas and she's really nervous about it. She said we could study at her house this weekend and I said okay. At least I know I won't binge while we're hanging out together anyway.

Love,
Judi

Dear Diary,

Monica and I studied this morning, then she practiced for a while and then about 3:00 we went to the mall because I had to get Mom a Chanukah present. Chanukah starts on December 9th. When I was little, I got a present all eight nights, but now me and Mom just give each other presents on the first night and the last night.

I didn't know what to get Mom and the mall was really crazy with Christmas shoppers. We went into all these stores and I couldn't find a thing. Monica suggested we try the bookstore and after browsing around for a minute, she came up with something she thought was perfect: a book of quotes by famous women. "She'll love it," Monica said, "and look, it's on sale, too."

"Just what I need," I groaned, "more expressions for Mom to throw at me." I opened the book and read the first saying that caught my eye: "To rest is to rust." "Forget it." I put the book back on its shelf and we left the bookstore. Finally I found something I thought Mom would like, a mug that says World's Greatest Mother on it. I know it's kind of corny, but Mom will love it. And I also got her this pretty scarf that isn't exactly silk but kind of feels like it. It's all purple and pink, her two favorite colors.

Monica approved of my presents, even though she still thought Mom would like the book of sayings better. Maybe I'll get it for her birthday next spring. I wonder what Mom's getting me. A while ago she said maybe she'd take me clothes shopping for Chanukah, but that was before I gained all my weight back. Oh well.

Love,
Judi

Dear Diary,

It's been a whole week since I made myself vomit, so I guess I'm cured. I should feel happy about it but I don't because I weigh 126 pounds, which is only 3½ pounds less than my all-time highest weight ever.

To tell you the truth, I didn't even feel like getting dressed today. Sometimes I wish I was in the hospital like Nancy Pratt, in a clean white bed with all these nurses hovering around in crisp white uniforms all ready to take care of me, and I wouldn't have to do anything at all.

Love,
Judi

Monday, December 5

Dear Diary,

Tests, tests, tests. And final papers. There should be a law against giving kids this much schoolwork. Fat chance of that ever happening, huh, Diary? If I survive the next two weeks and get everything done, it'll be a miracle. I hardly have a minute to write in you and I haven't even had time to go see Nancy Pratt, but I guess I'll swallow my pride and go tomorrow. This time I'm sure she'll say something about my weight. I'm back up to 127 pounds and I'm just blowing up like a balloon.

Love,

Judi

Dear Diary,

Well, I went to the hospital today and now I really don't know what to do. At first Nancy Pratt was really nice to me, saying what a good friend I was to visit her so much and she really appreciated it and all that. She even complimented me on my outfit (baggy jeans and old green sweater) and then she asked me to do her a favor.

"Listen, Judi," she said, "I want you to bring me some laxatives."

"What's the matter, are you constipated?" I asked her. "I'm sure the nurse has some."

"Never mind the nurse," Nancy Pratt said, and she gave me this look that said, *you're really stupid*, which I guess I am. Maybe a town somewhere would hire me as their village idiot. "If the nurse finds out, she'll kill me."

"But why?" I asked. "There's nothing wrong with being constipated."

"Judi, it's instead of this." She made our old secret signal with her fingers like she used to when she wanted me to meet her in the bathroom at school.

"Oh." Stupid me finally got it. "But Nancy, if you lose more weight, they'll never let you out of here. And you're definitely thin enough."

"You're just jealous of how good I look," she said, and for the first time, dear Diary, I realized that Nancy Pratt is really one sick cookie (no pun intended). I mean, who would be jealous of someone who looks like they just got out of a concentration camp?

Nancy Pratt kept waiting for me to say something and then when I didn't, she got mad. "Judi, of all people, I thought you would try to help me. You owe me, you know. If it wasn't for me, you'd still be fat."

I still am fat, I thought, but I guess that was beside the point. "What about your plan to gain the seven pounds and then lose them over Christmas vacation?" I asked.

"No good." She shook her head. "Bruce is taking me to a Christmas party and I've got to look good for that. Hey, maybe you and your boyfriend could come with us."

"Uh, we broke up," I said, which wasn't exactly true, since we were never really going out in the first place, but Nancy Pratt doesn't have to know that. "What if you don't get out of here in time?" I asked, anxious to change the subject.

"I'll get out. I'm not sure how yet, but I will. This place is making me crazy."

She shut her eyes as if that would make the hospital room disappear and I let out a sigh of relief. Of course Nancy Pratt wasn't going to ask what happened between me and my "boyfriend." She doesn't really care about anyone but herself.

I got up to go, and Nancy Pratt sat up, too. She reached down into her book bag and pulled out our math workbook. "Look." She opened it and there was this huge hole where she had ripped out the middle of a bunch of pages to make a hiding place. "Just hide the laxatives in there. No one will know, they'll just think you're bringing me my homework." She took out a piece of paper. "Here. I wrote down what I want. When do you think you'll be back?"

I looked down at the piece of paper. "I don't know, Nancy, I—"

"Judi." She stared right into my eyes and spoke in this sickeningly sweet voice. "You don't want the whole eighth grade to know what I know, do you? I can just hear Tommy Aristo calling you Barf Breath."

"He's not going to tease me anymore," I said. "He promised."

"You believe that?" Nancy Pratt laughed. "Well, I'm sure your mother wouldn't want to know what her darling daughter does."

"Give me that." I snatched the stupid piece of paper from Nancy Pratt and took her math workbook, too, just as a nurse came in.

"Thanks, Judi," Nancy Pratt said. "I'm having trouble with chapter six, so if you could just look over my workbook for me, that would be a big help. When do you think you'll be back?"

"On Saturday, I guess."

"Saturday? Can't you come before then? I really don't want to get behind on my schoolwork."

Forget about modeling, Diary. Nancy Pratt should have gone into acting. She deserves an Academy Award for her portrayal of a concerned junior high student.

"I'll try," I said, "but I have to help my mom around the house for the next couple of days," which is true, since I always have to help her.

So when I got home I read the piece of paper and it said, "Chocolate Ex-Lax. They have them at Morgan's Pharmacy. I knew I could count on you, Judi. What are friends for?"

Some friend, huh, Diary? I really feel sick, and for once in my life, it's not from too much food.

Love,

Judi

Wednesday, December 7

Dear Diary,

After school today I went to the drugstore for Nancy Pratt's laxatives. I just stood in the aisle and looked at them for a long time. There's lots of different kinds: natural laxatives, herbal laxatives, pills, powders, even wafers. Maybe I should try laxatives, too, Diary. They don't seem as dangerous as throwing up and I guess they help you lose weight because they move everything through your system faster. So I wound up buying two packages of laxatives—one for Nancy Pratt and one for me.

When I got home, I started feeling kind of weird about the whole thing, like being an accessory to the crime or something (I do not want to be a professional thief!). I mean, what if Nancy Pratt takes all these laxatives and dies? That would be so awful, and it would be all my fault.

So I decided the only thing for me to do was to take them first and see what happened. The directions said to take only one, but I took two since I'm sure that's what Nancy Pratt will do. Nothing happened for a while, but then my stomach started to hurt and then I got the runs like you wouldn't believe. It was really gross, but afterwards I was all right and I guess no one's ever died just from having diarrhea. Maybe I even lost a little weight from it, Diary. I'll let you know.

Love,
Judi

Thursday, December 8

Dear Diary,

I still weigh 127 pounds, even after taking the laxatives, so maybe they don't really work after all. Of course I could have lost some weight, but you'd never know because I'm sure the three pieces of chocolate cake I ate right afterwards put it right back on. Mom was out last night doing a Mary Kay appointment (she always has a lot of business during the holiday season) and Monica's phone was busy and I don't know, I guess I was just lonely, so I ate.

Today Paul Weinstein stopped me in the hall and asked me if I would look at some of his cartoons and help him come up with some captions for them. "I've been really stuck," he said, "and I know you could help me."

"Well, I don't know," I said, "I'm really busy until the end of the semester."

"Listen, Judi." He looked at me through his thick glasses. "I know you have a boyfriend and everything, so it's not like I'm asking you out. I'm just asking you to help me do this project."

It's funny, dear Diary, but when Paul Weinstein did ask me out, I didn't want to go with him, and now that he wasn't asking me out, I kind of wished that he would. "I don't have a boyfriend," I said, and then I looked away.

"You don't?" He looked down and I could see out of the corner of my eye that he was smiling. "Maybe you could come over during Christmas vacation and we could work on a comic book together."

"Okay," I said, and we both stood there looking down, like his sneakers and my old brown shoes were the two most fascinating things in the entire world.

At lunch I told Monica and she thought it was great. "When I was going out with The Rat," (that's our name for Richard Weiss) "every once in a while Paul would come along and he was always really nice. Sometimes I think the guys that aren't all that good-looking are really the nice ones after all."

"Yeah, I know what you mean." Wouldn't that be funny, Diary, if I had a real boyfriend before Monica? I mean, Richard Weiss was her boyfriend for a little while, but she said he was such a creep, he doesn't really count. I don't think I like Paul Weinstein "that way" but I did get this funny little happy feeling when he asked me to come over to his house during Christmas vacation. I don't know, but I guess as Mom would say, "time will tell." One thing I did think of is if Paul Weinstein ever did kiss me, he'd probably take his glasses off, which would be an improvement.

Only one more week of school and then it'll be Christmas vacation. Today in English Ms. Roth reminded us to write a one-page summary of our diaries and a list of insights we've learned about ourselves. I think it'll be interesting to go back and read you, Diary. We've been through so much together.

Love,

Judi

<u>Friday, December 9</u>

Dear Diary,

Happy Chanukah! Mom came home early from work so we could light the menorah together at sunset. She took it down from the china closet where she keeps it and polished it up with a special cloth. Our menorah is really pretty. It's silver, and it looks like a tree, with nine branches to hold all the candles. Mom got the menorah as a wedding present so she always cries when we light it and say the blessing and tonight was no exception. Luckily the phone rang right when we were done. It was Grandma, calling to wish us a happy Chanukah.

"Did you get our card, darling?" she asked me.

"Not yet, Grandma."

"Well, there's a little Chanukah gelt in there for you," she said, "and I want you to use it to buy something nice for yourself. And then maybe you'll come down and show us what you picked out, we haven't seen you in such a long time."

"We'll see you soon, Grandma," I said.

"Tell your mother she should bring you down here so your grandparents don't forget what their own grand-daughter looks like."

"You tell her, Grandma, here, I'll put her on." What's a little gelt without a little guilt? I thought, and then I handed the phone to Mom and wrote down gelt/guilt so I'd remember to tell Paul Weinstein. I bet he could draw a really funny cartoon to go with that caption. Speaking of Paul Weinstein, he gave me a Chanukah present today, too. Well, it wasn't really a present, it was a card, but he drew the whole thing himself, so it is kind of special. It wasn't a cartoon, it was a real drawing of a beautiful menorah with all the candles. I bet Paul Weinstein will be a famous artist and a famous cartoonist someday, and I can't think of even one thing I want to be, let alone two.

194

Finally I heard Mom promise Grandpa in a loud voice that we would definitely come down to Florida for Passover and then she hung up and it was time to give each other our presents.

I gave Mom her World's Greatest Mother mug and she loved it like I knew she would. She said she's going to drink her after-supper cup of coffee out of it every single night. And guess what she gave me—Chanukah gelt to buy myself a whole new outfit. Too bad I'm fat again, but maybe I'll buy myself something new anyway. I can't decide.

"I know it's not a very personal present," Mom said, "but when I went to the store, I couldn't find anything I was sure you would like. You're growing up and changing so fast, Judi, it's like I hardly know you anymore."

"That's okay, Mom, you're still the World's Greatest Mother," I said, and then she got all weepy again.

"It's a good thing you sell Mary Kay cosmetics," I said to Mom as she dabbed at her eyes.

"Why?"

"Because if you didn't know a lot about makeup, you probably wouldn't be wearing waterproof mascara and you'd have black circles under your eyes like a raccoon." That made Mom laugh.

"Judi, when the holidays are over, things will ease up for me and one of my New Year's resolutions is to spend more time with you. Does that sound okay?"

"Sure," I said, and I made her some coffee in her new mug. When I gave it to her, she stared at me with That Look in her eye—you know what I mean, dear Diary, the way she gets all sentimental and misty looking. "I'm very proud of you, Judi," she said. "You're getting very grown up and even though you're quiet and a little mysterious sometimes, I know I never have to worry about you. You hear all kinds of stories about the crazy things teenagers do these days, but I know you're too smart to ever get yourself into serious trouble."

Oh, Diary, if Mom only knew! I would just die if Nancy Pratt ever told her anything. Mom would be *so* disappointed in me.

Anyway, then Mom made latkes, another Jewish tradition having to do with food. I grated like a million potatoes, which was exhausting even though I'm sure it did burn up some calories, and Mom fried them up. You're supposed to eat greasy foods on Chanukah to symbolize the holy oil that burned for eight days, thousands of years ago. I don't think the oil in Mom's frying pan was holy or anything, but it sure was noisy, sizzling and sputtering around the raw potatoes. At least we didn't set off the fire alarm like we did last year.

When we sat down to eat, Mom said, "Umm, these latkes are so good, we should have them more than once a year." But thank God we don't, dear Diary. They are *so* fattening! We eat them with applesauce and sour cream, which just adds more calories. And I ate five, so I just had to throw up afterwards. I'm sure they're at least 500 calories each, and I just couldn't face Nancy Pratt tomorrow if I gained another ounce. I took two laxatives, too, which was pretty awful.

The Chanukah card Mom got me said, "May your

life be full of miracles." I wish God would make a miracle and take this problem away.

Love,

Judi

Dear Diary,

I went to see Nancy Pratt today. A really cute nurse was taking her blood pressure and as soon as he left the room, she whispered, "Did you get it?" I swear, I felt like a drug dealer, which is certainly not a profession I'm anxious to get into.

"I got it," I said slowly, "but Nancy, I don't know, do you really think it's such a good idea?"

"Give it," she said, holding out her hand.

I still hesitated and she got mad. "You better give it to me, Judi Liebowitz," she said, "or I'll turn the entire junior high school against you. You know I can do it, too. Plus, I'll tell your mother everything, and I mean *everything*. Now, do you want to be my friend, or not?"

All I could think of was last night when Mom said how proud of me she was, Diary, and how I couldn't stand to ruin that. So I just gave Nancy Pratt her math workbook. She grabbed it and looked inside and when she saw I had hidden the laxatives in the hole she had ripped out, she smiled and said, "Thanks, Judi."

"Are you going to take them now?" I whispered.

197

"No, I'm going to wait until after supper, since that's the heaviest meal of the day and they make me eat the whole thing. And I have to be careful, the nurses are always looking in here." She turned away. "You better go now. I'm supposed to rest."

So I left, but I'm really, really worried about her and I really don't feel like visiting her again. What if she asks me to bring her more laxatives, or what if she makes me help her sneak out of there? Another thing I don't want to be is a kidnapper. I don't know what to do, dear Diary. I sure wish you could tell me.

Love,
Judi

Sunday, December 11

Dear Diary,

Today I spent the whole day reading everything I wrote in you since the first day of school. Boy, did I write a lot. Mostly stuff about my weight problem, and how I tried to solve it, but other stuff, too, like about my crushes on Richard Weiss and Michael Silver and my fight with Monica. And stuff about Mom and even a little bit about my dad, too.

And then I made a list of all the jobs I've ruled out in my never-ending search of what I want to be when I grow up. Here's what I've decided I *don't* want to be, or I'm not smart enough to be:

model
fashion designer
mathematician
rock and roll star
hairdresser
kindergarten teacher
psychic
rabbi
politician
camp counselor
full-time mom
athlete
gym teacher
page turner for a musician
movie director
fat lady in a circus
librarian
actress
bookstore clerk
aerobics instructor
weatherperson
carpenter
telephone operator
doorperson
high school English teacher
bodyguard
EMT (emergency medical technician)
doctor or nurse or any other hospital job
chef
waitress

counselor (not camp counselor, therapist kind of
     counselor)
village idiot
thief
drug dealer
kidnapper

Well, that's all that I don't want to be, and I still don't
know what I *do* want to be, which isn't much of an
insight.

One thing I noticed is that when I started my diary I
weighed 127 pounds, and now four months later, even
after everything that's happened, I still weigh 127
pounds. Do you think that counts as an insight, Diary?
And another thing I noticed is that the days I weighed
120 pounds, I didn't sound one bit happier than the days
I weighed 129½. I still worried about my weight, I still
didn't have a boyfriend, and I still had no idea what I
wanted to do with my life.

The other thing I've been thinking about of course is
Nancy Pratt. First I was totally jealous of her for being
so thin and everything, and then I discovered her
"beauty secret" and now I don't envy her at all. She is
really too thin, which is something I never thought was
possible. It wasn't really right of me to give her those
laxatives yesterday.

But guess what, Diary? Remember I wrote yesterday
that I wished you could tell me what to do? Well, you
did! It was right there in my own handwriting, on November 28th (is that what Mom means when she says

the writing is on the wall?). Anyway, it was after that assembly when I was asking Miss Fiorino about my "bulimic friend" and she said, "If your friend's life was in danger, don't you think telling an adult would be the right thing to do?" Nancy Pratt's not exactly my friend, dear Diary, I can see now that she's been using me all along, but still, I don't want her to die or anything. So I'm going to have to tell someone. It's not going to be easy and she'll probably hate my guts forever, but I know I have to do it. Wish me luck.

Love,
Judi

Monday, December 12

Dear Diary,

Today after my last class I went to the English room and asked Ms. Roth if I could talk to her. She said of course, and after everyone else had left, she closed the door and asked me, "What's on your heart?" instead of "What's on your mind?" I thought that was pretty funny, dear Diary, only instead of laughing, guess what? I started to cry.

Then when I could catch my breath, I told Ms. Roth *everything*. I didn't mean to. I was just going to tell her about Nancy Pratt and the laxatives (which would be a very sick name for a punk rock band, come to think of it). But once I started talking, I just couldn't stop, and the more I talked, the more I cried. Ms. Roth put her arms around me and gave me a big hug and for a minute I was afraid that Tommy Aristo would barge in and say, "What's this, a Ms. Piggy Crying Convention?" but then I remembered he promised he wouldn't tease me anymore, and anyway, I was too upset to care.

After I finally calmed down, I felt really relieved, like someone had taken this tremendous weight off my shoulders, but then I got scared that Ms. Roth would get mad at me for giving Nancy Pratt the Ex-Lax.

But Ms. Roth was great. She got me some tissues from the top drawer of her desk and she didn't yell at me at all.

"That was very brave of you, Judi, to come and tell me everything," she said. "I'm glad you felt you could trust me. Now, let's make a plan."

"What kind of plan?" I asked.

"Let's see." Ms. Roth sat down at her desk and I pulled up a chair next to her. "First of all, you have to tell someone at the hospital about the laxatives."

I knew she was going to say that, and I know she's right, even though I'm sure Nancy Pratt will never talk to me again. I just hope she doesn't tell the entire eighth grade about my little problem.

"Is there anyone at the hospital you can talk to?" Ms. Roth asked.

"Well, there's this one nurse there who seems kind of nice," I said, thinking of the young one with three earrings that I've seen a few times. "I guess I could talk to her."

"Good." Ms. Roth looked down at her hands and

then looked up at me. "Now, what about you, Judi? Do you think you can talk to your mom about this?"

"I don't know," I said, and my chin started shaking like I was going to cry again. "She'll be so disappointed in me. But I'm afraid if I don't tell her, I'll wind up in the hospital like Nancy Pratt."

"I don't think that will happen," Ms. Roth said, "but it would probably be a good idea for you to see a counselor once or twice a week, just so you can have someone to really talk to. It's hard to get better all by yourself." Then she looked down at her hands again and said, "Judi, I probably shouldn't tell you this, but I used to be bulimic, too."

"But you're fat!" I blurted out, and then I was really embarrassed. I'm sure I turned beet red, but Ms. Roth just shrugged. "So, I'm fat," she said. "It's okay, Judi, you didn't insult me. It's just like saying, 'You're tall.' I know I'm fat and I don't really mind."

"You don't?" I looked at her in complete amazement. "You really don't wish that you were thin?"

She shook her head. "I used to," she said. "I tried every diet I could think of, but nothing ever worked. I would lose weight, but it always came right back. So I finally decided that this must be the body I was meant to have and I just accepted it. It's a perfectly good body. I just wish the world was a gentler place, and people weren't mean to those of us who happen to be fat." She looked a little sad.

"But wouldn't you be happier if you were thin?" I asked.

Ms. Roth shook her head. "I'm very happy with my

life, Judi. I have a job that means something to me, a husband who loves me, and a wonderful baby daughter. What more could I want?"

Wow, I didn't know Ms. Roth was a mother!

"There's more important things in life than a twenty-inch waist," Ms. Roth said. "I know you don't believe that now," she added, like she was reading my mind, "but maybe someday you will. And speaking of more important things, how else has the semester been?"

"Okay, I guess." I didn't know what to say. I mean, I certainly didn't want to tell Ms. Roth about my love life. "I don't know, Ms. Roth. I don't like my classes all that much. I don't really have any interests, like my best friend Monica is really into music and Paul Weinstein is really into drawing, and I don't know, I can't think of anything that I want to do."

"Well." Ms. Roth thought for a minute. "How do you spend your time? What do you like to do? Outside of school, I mean."

"Nothing, really." I felt so dumb. "I mean, me and Monica hang out at the mall and stuff, but that's about it. The only thing I really like doing is writing in my diary. Look." I fished my journal out of my bag and flipped through it. "I wrote all this."

"Well then, Judi, the answer is simple. Maybe you want to be a writer."

"A writer? You mean and write books?"

Ms. Roth laughed. "Yes, unless you can think of other things writers write."

I just stared at her. "But do you really think I could be?"

"I don't see why not. One of the most important things about persuing an art form is discipline, and you seem to have plenty of that."

"Wow." I couldn't believe Ms. Roth thought I was actually smart enough to be a writer. "Paul Weinstein thinks I'm really good with words, Ms. Roth. Sometimes I help him make up captions for his cartoons and we're going to work on a comic book together over Christmas vacation."

"You see, you're on your way already. I'd like to see what you two come up with." Then she stood up and put her hands on her hips. "Judi," she said, "can I ask you a serious question?"

I was a little nervous, but I said sure.

"Do you think I'm a good teacher?"

"Of course. You're the best!"

"Do you think I'd be a better teacher if I lost ten pounds?"

I laughed. "What difference would that make?"

"Think about that," Ms. Roth said, and then I went home. What do you make of all this, dear Diary?

Love,

Judi

<u>Tuesday, December 13</u>

Dear Diary,

Today I went to the hospital right after school. I couldn't go yesterday on account of staying after school and talking to Ms. Roth for so long. When I walked into Nancy Pratt's room, she wasn't there. At first I thought she was down the hall talking to her counselor or something, but then I noticed that some of her things were gone—you know her cards from Bruce that used to be all over her night table and stuff. Then I thought maybe she went home, but if she did, all her stuff would be gone, not just some of it, and then I thought maybe she ran away and took only what she thought was important, which of course would be the cards from Bruce. Then I had this horrible thought: what if Nancy Pratt had died? I was just standing there staring at her bed and feeling kind of shaky when I heard someone come in. It was the nurse with the three earrings.

"Are you looking for your friend?" she asked.

I nodded my head because I was too scared to speak.

"She checked out yesterday."

"Did she go home?"

"No," the nurse said. "She's been on a waiting list for a residential eating disorders clinic and a spot finally opened up for her. I think it'll be better for her there, where she can get the care and supervision she needs." The nurse put her hands on her hips and shook her head, which made all three of her earrings swing. "A young girl like that, it's a pity. She has everything—parents who love her, a handsome boyfriend—I can't imagine why a girl would do that to herself, can you?"

I can only imagine too well, dear Diary. "What about her stuff?" I asked.

"I was just gathering up her things," the nurse said. "Her parents said they'd come back this evening to pick up everything."

"Can I take her math workbook?" I asked, trying to sound casual. "I was supposed to pick it up today and bring it to our teacher."

"Go ahead," the nurse said, and I just took that book and ran home as fast as I could. I was really scared to look inside, dear Diary, but when I did I found the laxatives were still in there, and the package wasn't even open. Nancy Pratt probably had to go before she had a chance to take any, thank God. I am going to destroy the evidence, and I am never, *never* going to do anything that stupid again.

Love,

Judi

Wednesday, December 14

Dear Diary,

Today after school, I went over to Monica's house and she gave me my own private concert of the solo she's going to play at her recital. It was like a dress rehearsal because she put on her performance clothes and everything, and when she was done I yelled "Bravo!" and gave her a standing ovation. Then I did something that was really hard to do. I went over to Monica and sat down next to her on the piano bench.

"Wanna sing some Whitney Houston songs?" she asked.

"No," I said, "I have something to tell you."

"What?"

"Well." I couldn't look at her, so I kept my eyes down on the black and white keys. "I made myself throw up," I said, in a really tiny voice.

"Judi, you promised!"

"I know." I kept my eye on middle C. "I'm sorry. Do you think I'm a horrible person?" I asked.

"No," she said, "I think you're a horrible promise keeper."

"I'm sorry," I said again. "Do you still want to be my friend?"

"No," Monica said, and I looked up, shocked. Monica didn't say anything more, so I got up off the bench. "I don't blame you," I said, starting for the door. "I guess I'll just go."

"Judi, you are so dense!" Monica jumped up, too. "I don't want to be your friend, you goon. I want to be your *best* friend."

"Really?" I turned around. "You don't think I'm too disgusting to be friends with?"

"No." Monica shook her head. "I think too highly of myself to be best friends with a disgusting person," she said, and I had to smile. "But Judi, I'm worried about you, and I want you to get some help."

"I will, Monica. I promise."

At the word "promise," Monica raised one eyebrow. "All right, I swear," I said, and Monica raised her other eyebrow. "Wanna shake on it?" I asked, coming toward her, and this time Monica raised both her eyebrows. "All right, what?"

"Just get some help," Monica said, "and don't insult me again by thinking I don't want to be your best friend."

"Monica, you're the best," I said, and I gave her a big hug and of course I started to cry then, so we went into the kitchen to get a napkin so I could blow my nose and then I went home.

Tonight after we lit the Chanukah candles, I asked Mom if I could give her her present, even though it wasn't the last night when we usually do it. She said okay, if I *really* couldn't wait. I told her no, I really couldn't, so I gave her a box and she opened it. Inside was the pink-and-purple scarf I bought at the mall and guess what it was wrapped around? You, dear Diary, which is why I'm writing this on a scrap of loose-leaf paper.

Mom lifted you out and turned to the first page. "This is your diary, Judi," she said, as if I didn't know. "You want me to read it?"

"Sure," I said, trying to sound really casual. "You're always saying you feel like you don't know me, so now I'm giving you the story of my life."

Mom got all weepy and gave me a big hug and said she wanted to give me my present, too. And guess what it was, dear Diary? A complete makeup kit, with eyeliner and eye shadow and mascara and blush and lipstick and everything!

"Wow!" I said. "This is the best present in the world."

"No, this is the best present in the world," Mom said, holding you up, dear Diary. I hope she still thinks so, after she reads you.

Love,
Judi

P.S. I hope it's okay with you, dear Diary, that I'm letting Mom read you. I just couldn't think of any other way to tell her everything.

P.P.S. Don't worry, Diary, Mom knows she doesn't get to keep you, and she promises she'll give you back to me as soon as she's done. But she does get to keep the scarf.

Thursday, December 15

Dear Diary,

Tonight after I did the dishes and made Mom her after-supper cup of coffee, I went upstairs to my room to do my homework and there you were, right on my pillow. You weren't there when I got home from school, so I guess Mom must have put you there before supper when she went upstairs to take off her shoes.

Anyway, there was a bookmark inside you so I turned to the page that was marked, and guess what—Mom had written me a letter. I hope you don't mind. This is what it said:

Dear Judi,
    Last night I stayed up reading your diary until I just couldn't keep my eyes open anymore, and then today on my lunch hour I finished reading the whole thing. I just couldn't put it down and I'm very impressed. You have a very vivid imagination and a wonderful way with words and I'm sure you are going to be a very famous writer someday.
    I want you to know something. You are my wonderful, smart, beautiful, talented daughter and I love you very much, more than anything or anyone in the whole wide world. I will always love you and be proud of you, no matter how much you weigh. You could weigh 97 pounds or 127 pounds or 227 pounds and it wouldn't matter. What does matter is that you are happy, and I'm very sorry you've been so troubled all fall and you didn't feel that you could tell me about it. I love you and I am proud of you and I am not ashamed of you and I am not angry at you. I am honored that you gave me your diary to read and I promise you we will work this out together.
    Thank you for letting me in, Judi. Always

remember, my beautiful daughter, that I love you very, very, very, very, *very* much, and nothing in the world will ever, ever change that.

Mom

I read the note over and over and in case you're wondering what those splotches on some of the words are, well, I cried a little bit, too. I mean, I can't believe that Mom's not mad at me. And I always knew that she loved me, but she never wrote it in a note like that before.

Then Mom came upstairs and she hugged me real tight and we both cried some and then she said she made an appointment with a therapist for me tomorrow. Mom's even taking the day off from work so she can take me and she's even letting me miss school, which is no big deal, really, since we never do anything the day before Christmas break anyway.

I wonder what going to a therapist is going to be like. I'll let you know all about it tomorrow, Diary. I'm glad Mom read you, and I'm glad to have you back.

Love,
Judi

Friday, December 16

Dear Diary,

Mom took me to my therapy appointment today. She stayed in the waiting room and I went into the therapist's office, and guess who was in there waiting for me: Miss Fiorino! I guess after Mom read about her in you, dear Diary, she tracked down the clinic Miss Fiorino works at through school. Anyway, I was really surprised to see Miss Fiorino, but she didn't seem surprised to see me at all. I was afraid she was going to ask me how my "friend" was, but she didn't. She just smiled and said, "It's nice to see you, Judi. Why don't you sit over there?" and pointed to a couch. Then she sat down on a chair across from me and asked me to tell her all about my eating, so I did.

"Do you think I can get better?" I asked, when I was done.

"Do you want to?" she asked, tapping the tips of her fingers together. Today her nails were painted hot pink.

"Of course I want to," I said.

"Then most likely, you will," Miss Fiorino said. "I've worked with lots of girls your age and most of them have been very successful."

"What do you mean by successful?" I asked.

"What would success mean to you?" she asked back.

I thought about that for a minute. "I guess not throwing up anymore," I said, but then this feeling of panic started bubbling in my stomach. "But do you think if I stop throwing up, I'll gain a lot of weight?"

"Does that scare you?" Miss Fiorino asked. She never answers a question except by asking another one.

"Yes."

"Well, Judi." Miss Fiorino looked at me with her green eyes. "There's a slim chance that you'll gain a small amount of weight while your body starts to heal, but who knows? Once you let your body develop naturally and you learn to eat according to your own physical hunger instead of according to a diet, it's very possible that you'll end up with a body that you really like."

"Fat chance!" I said, and then I started to laugh. Miss Fiorino wanted to know what was so funny and I told her and I'm telling you, Diary, and I'm going to write Ms. Roth and tell her, too, because here's the one true insight I learned about myself this semester: I finally figured out that a fat chance and a slim chance are really the very same thing.

Love and kisses,

Judi